I0623820

ARETTA'S
GIFT

BY

MARK J GRAVER

AND

OSIRIS INDEPENDENT PRESS
AFTON, VA 22920

-EST 2011-

to the sanguine woman

© Copyright 2011 by Mark Graver

All rights reserved, which includes the right of reproduction in whole or in part in any form.

Library of Congress Control Number: 2012900270

ISBN-13: 978-0-9834947-1-3

ISBN-10: 0-9834947-1-3

Osiris Independent Press can be visited via the following web address: www.osirispress.com

or email: markjohngraver@hotmail.com

– In memory of Esharah Liana Graver
whose short and courageous life sparked the story
that is about to unfold

I

THE QUESTION

Once, in the beautiful land of Lydia there ruled a queen both fair and virtuous. So fair and virtuous was she that she was loath to do any foul deed however large or small. Even the mice who came to her castle could feel quite free from harm. Not only that, but she was also loath to be caught doing anything other than that which was seemly and right. Every moment of the day for her was like a dance where each and every action contained the graceful beauty found in virtue and excellence. This lovely queen, Aretta, ruled alongside her husband, Thaddeus, a man renowned for his justice, understanding, and gentleness. Together, the kingdom flourished in peace and harmony.

Eventually, with the kingdom at peace, the royal couple decided to start a family, to bear children who would walk in their steps, and to thus leave behind for the people of Lydia, a legacy of leaders who would love the Lydians as much as they did.

However, late one winter night, while the full moon hung high overhead, filling the clear sky with her chilling glow and below, the refractions of pale moonlight danced from hill to hill upon the still and frozen snow covered land, Queen Aretta slept a restless sleep.

As she tossed and turned, a transformation was taking place inside her body and during that transformation, she had a dream. Upon a lofty hill, she watched as the land of Lydia crumbled into ruin. The gentle rolling hills of green meadow grass fell away bit by bit, and rising in their place was an enormous and terrible tower, whose jagged edges and magnitude evoked feelings of fear and hostility. Fire burned in every direction, and as she watched, her beloved town of Asralon came into view. Suddenly, she saw that that terrible tower was looming over the edge of Asralon and standing exactly where her castle stood: the very place in which she then laid! A terrible realization came over her and filled her with terror, upon which, suddenly, as the shot of a cannon, a voice boomed forth from the storm-filled sky, which looked all the more menacing as a circle of smoke rose from the smouldering high-lands and forests all around. The voice called out loudly and deliberately as it said, "Rise, my daughter! Make haste! There is still time! Yes, tonight you have conceived and you will give birth to a son. But we have seen that his deeds shall be terrible and his heart shall be darker than smoke. In his wickedness, he shall lay waste your beloved land till there is nothing left, and no man shall be able to stop him!"

Yet the voice continued, more consolingly, "But, do not despair. He can be stopped now; and naught shall ever come of it, nor shall any suffer harm. By the river, this night, grows a vine bearing berries of a twisted form and orange colour. Whoever eats this berry suffers no harm, but by this means can you bring death to him who grows within."

The voice then pressed more urgently: "Go, Now! Run! And as a sign that these things are so, the river will stand motionless upon your arrival while the grim sight of your unborn son's misdeeds will be seen in the stilled stream."

Sitting straight up in her bed, Queen Aretta awoke with sudden-ness from her dream, her eyes full of tears, and straightway, she became filled with one thought. Urgency filled her heart, and that one thought sent her running through the palace stricken with panic and grief.

From her chamber, she raced down the long circling stairs of the royal tower. At the bottom, she made a quick right and went down the double staircase whose second set turned left toward an underpass near the royal stables. Getting outside at the base of those stairs, she looked left and then right (both sides went toward the stream, which made a large loop around the southern tower of the castle: to the left or west, lay the western pine forest, to the east or right, lay Asralon), upon which she precipitately went that direction, past the stables and toward the bridge to Asralon. Heading straight for the stream, she ran with all her heart, sparing neither life nor limb, as her naked feet pierced through the frosty ice covered snow with every forceful step.

After a hundred yards, she reached the crest of the hill that descended sharply toward the stream. From there the overall lay of the town of Asralon could be seen through the then bare treetops that lined the riverbank, and flicks of candlelight cast a soft eerie aureola against the frost-covered windows of some of the homes. Aretta advanced though, like a vanguard foot soldier blindly storming an enemy stronghold. The icy snow tore open her soft, smooth skin as she pressed herself ferally down the hill: first tumbling here, then slipping there. She neared the banks and began to see the bluish, iridescent light of the full moon, now at her summit, bouncing in the rapids of the river Sheaglow, through the thick but barren brush. She forced her way through the brush and followed the smooth river stones near the river's edge. Frantically, she looked about in hopes of satisfying that one thought, when her eyes beheld and became transfixed by the numinous sign: the stream came to a halt and her dream image formed in the stilling waters. At the sight of it, she stepped back in terror, and in so doing, a thorn sank into her shoulder. Her discomfort gave way to wonder after turning to face the briars, when her eyes caught the moonlight glimmering upon the shiny surface of an orange coloured berry.

The berry gently shimmied during the disturbance and reminded her of a small, elongated bell in the way it bounced, suspended as though from a thread, and caught the light of the moon. Hurriedly, like a paladin, she seized it at once, and though trembling violently, she lifted it toward her mouth. Then suddenly, she stood there motionless until other tears began to flow from her eyes. 'Why should it have come to this?' she thought. 'What wrong have I done to be dealt such a severe charge?' She turned toward the scene in the river as the kingdom of Lydia crumbled before her eyes. She then muttered audibly and forcibly to herself, "If you do not do this, I will force it upon you."

She stood still once again, desperately fixed upon the terrible images of her dream, searching for courage. Thereupon, she took a shallow breath and through her nose, now choked up with tears, she gave a decided snuff, after which, she slowly opened her hand and let the twisted orange berry fall to the ground. She broke out in tears once again and sobbing profusely, she repeatedly mouthed the words, "I cannot take the life of my unborn child...."

Just then, the stream began to flow, and overhead Venus seemed to counterchange positions with the Moon. Further unknown to her, on the other side of the river, slept an unprincipled merchant who after hearing the clamor lay awake and witnessed everything. After about an hour had passed following the queen's departure from the riverbank, he crossed the nearby bridge and made a careful search to understand the events of the night.

II

ANOTHER LIGHT

Meanwhile, across the river, the streets of Asralon lay covered with snow, and a quiet, poor and simple mother slept a restless sleep. The sleepy town was filled with a chilling silence as the snow, blown by the wind, raced up and down her narrow streets. And lo! Except for those few flickers of candlelight, one would think the town had not a soul in her. In the south side of town, this mother laid, Anna, a widow, nine-months pregnant, and restless indeed; filled she was with grief and stricken with fear.

She was a middle-aged woman, sapped and completely spent, having not eaten more than meager crumbs for several weeks, a woman bereaved of both husband and company. She knew her time would come and that she would bring into this world a brand new life that would come crying and begging for sustentation, yet she had nothing. After many hours of wrestling her hopelessness and despairing for her life, she, totally exhausted, fell into a deep sleep.

Then, Bam! A strong gust of wind slammed the shutters against her house. She awoke in panic firstly, followed quickly by anger, and as the darkest thoughts began to fill her mind, she screamed out loud, "Oh, just killllllll mee!" Repeatedly she begged with tears until she could bear it no longer, for no one would answer. She felt utterly helpless and utterly alone. Closing her eyes, she took a deep breath, and then … and then … she faded away, ever so slowly, ever so gently. All the walls fell away from around her, and in the dark electrical world she found herself in, she heard a faint susurration. "Take courage child," the voice whispered, "it isn't over yet."

As Anna felt her surroundings slowly taking shape, this surreal gnosis reverberated deep within her, endowing her with new life and courage, until, at last, she opened her eyes. Suddenly, she no longer felt alone, and an extraordinary strength filled her. The moon had just passed its zenith, and moments later, her labour pains set on.

Now galvanized, her first two stages progressed relatively propitiously, a matter for which she was quite thankful. But in her final stage, she cried out in agony, when suddenly, the door swung open, and in came a tall, self-assured man in his middle ages. "Hal!" cried Anna. "Get your but over here!"

Hal didn't miss a beat: something in him just took over. It was as if every move he made was rehearsed, and Anna subsequently gave her heart to him. Besides, he loved being helpful, and there at her bedside, he had the joy of becoming Anna's heaven sent midwife and delivering his own niece. As the head of his kin emerged, he smiled broadly. His smile turned into an excited breathless laughter until Anna hollered, "I'm still here!" Hal quickly put on a serious face, and soon enough both of them were smiling in ecstasy, as he exalted the child and lifted her into the cold night air. Brimming with delight, he carefully positioned his beloved niece close to the breast of her mother, and she quickly suckled.

"So," said Hal, "what are you going to name her?"

"Luna," said Anna in her star-struck euphoria.

"Are you serious?" replied Hal.

"Yes," said Anna as she looked at the mysterious ethereal beauty of the moonlight. "I feel like new rays of light are finally upon me …" she turned to look at Luna and quietly said, "…us."

Hal offered Anna his bread and some wine and they both quickly fell asleep and slept with an enduring peace.

III

A HARD ROAD

Back at the palace, King Thaddeus had grown concerned for his beloved Aretta. After she flew out of the castle in such haste, he anxiously awaited her return. He determined that it was best to wait for Aretta to return when she was ready and share her troubles then, but his anxiety for Aretta bit no less fiercely. After waiting for quite some time, he began to fear for her safety, for he had not permitted the guards to follow her down. He could wait no longer. He made his descent accompanied by several guards; and taking a torch from a sconce in the wall, he followed her footprints toward the river. He soon began to see drops of blood spilt upon the snow-white ground near her footfalls.

When he got to the river, he saw a tall shadowy figure scurrying away. By the height he could tell it wasn't Aretta and he shouted for the figure to stop. Some of the guards broke away and gave chase, while King Thaddeus kept following Aretta's tracks. She had taken the road back to the castle. So, running, he passed the stalls on their northern side and followed the eastern side of the castle northerly. He soon reached the outer serenity gardens and followed her tracks into the inner marble courtyard enclosure. There among the ghastly monuments of kings and nobles of old, benches and fountains, and neatly groomed snow-covered evergreen shrubs, he saw her.

On the south side, in the center, near a great black marble monolith, she knelt trembling. He slowly came to her side, and her cold pale form slowly came into view. Coming around and facing her, he placed his left arm around her and felt her icy skin. Finding her nearly unresponsive, he lifted her and rushed her frozen body into the inner sanctuary, the entrance to which was nestled in a small alcove along the western wall of the inner courtyard.

By the warm firelight in the sanctuary, he could see her blue lips, her ghostly face, and her sunken and sorrowful eyes. Speechless, Thaddeus looked intently at his cherished wife. He caught a faint glimmer in her eyes as she looked back like a ghost inside a machine. As she slowly thawed, her lips began to quiver, and she took a strong deep breath. Then, she blinked, and suddenly, a slight warmth seemed to return to her mortified countenance. Soon after, her body began to tremble violently; so Thaddeus laid her near the fire and quickly covered her in dry blankets from near the hearth.

She said quietly, "I'm s-or-rr-y. I'm s-or-rr-y." Thereupon, her frown swallowed her face, and wells of tears filled her eyes.

The healer who was summoned by the guards shortly after the king saw Aretta's blood in the snow soon located the king and queen. He used his arts to invoke the Queen's guardians and restore her balance. During these first few hours, her condition was critical. Thaddeus held her tightly as the two of them sat together in silence with the healer standing by.

As the dawn ascended, Aretta recovered enough strength to raise herself up, and slowly, she walked toward a small window just to the left of the fireplace to watch the sun rising in the eastern gorge. She was still pale and detached, yet consoled. It seemed that whenever Thaddeus was near, she found an unknown strength. However great she could be, the stature of Thaddeus always seemed to surpass hers, reaching the status of nearly a god at times to her. The clouds of her consternation visibly began to clear, and as the last vestige dissipated, a warm smile melted through her previously stone-cold expression. Thaddeus then extended his arm to her, and she quickly took hold of it. Holding each other close for a few moments, Aretta pulled at her husband's arm, signaling her desire to leave the sanctuary. Arm and arm they quietly walked across the inner courtyard alone.

Leaving the courtyard through the northern archway, they began their walk through the outer gardens. There, Aretta confessed the whole matter to her husband who listened with great understanding, fully apprehending the magnitude of the charge given to her. After hearing her fully, he said reassuringly, "I'm going to be a father. And I will love this child like I love no other."

Their thoughts soon turned to the years of child rearing that lay ahead, and Thaddeus began talking about all of the things he could do together with his son. Lightening the mood, he said playfully, "But no diapers, I can't change diapers."

"Well that's what the servants are for," she chided as she nudged him with her elbow.

"Another bill, *oh*, the finance minister will be up in arms."

"And don't forget about the cost of decorating the nursery," Aretta added.

"They'll have me eating potatoes for a year."

After a long pause, he added, "Quite a little prankster we've found in that devil, life! What in the world is this thing called perfection if we never are meant to have it?"

"That's it – perfection," Aretta mocked, "perhaps we could show this boy a world in which not a single rotten, vile thing existed. Then he'll never know what sort of trouble he could cause even if he wanted to."

But deep inside, they both knew that there would be days when Aretta's heart would nearly break for not having taken his life, and justification for having spared him would nowhere be found. Thaddeus was determined to be there for her at those impossible junctures, when Aretta would come face to face with the disastrous truth that lay ahead. He wanted to tell her to be strong or offer some other word of encouragement, but all he could do was continue holding her.

IV

SIXTEEN CANDLES

The days went by quickly, and soon enough Aretta gave birth to a son whom they named Nathan. Nathan was a very "normal" child, and his childhood years passed quickly. In all things, Aretta tried to instill her gentle and peaceful ways into her son. Nathan followed suit and readily assented to the ways of his father and mother. He could sometimes be found distributing food to the needy, playing games with the children who frequented the palace, or offering to help with diverse chores, but he always loved a good adventure with his father or a smile of approval from his mother. And his favorite companion by far, was his uncle, Obstitrix, Thaddeus' brother, who was a sort of a sage.

Obstitrix was a somewhat short, healthy, stalwart quinquagenarian who was entrusted with the education of the prince. Among other things, they went on hunts, where Nathan became a masterful marksman. They often spent several days on their hunts and came home with tales of extraordinary adventures of scaling cliffs and getting fairly lost in caves and forests across the land.

Except for Obstitrix, who also advised the king and queen, no one in all the land knew of the dark secret that they anxiously kept. Obstitrix, however, was too wise to care. Being a man of his own, he found solace in the works of the ancient philosophers and could often be found with Nathan by his side, poring over the tattered copies that rested in the more secret vaults of the library. For him, hope was too naïve; and fear, the obstinacy of a desperate mind. He ultimately believed that the forces of nature were as blind as he was while at the same time exacting justice with the tenuous skill of a gambler.

In those days, the Lydians enjoyed an equal and balanced social structure, where each Lydian felt assured that their every need would somehow be met. Thaddeus and Aretta increased in wealth and favor, and managed the nation's abundant resources with love and compassion. All surplus food and wealth was reverently shared with the people of Lydia. At each of the national festivals, the populace exuberantly feasted and congratulated one another. Generosity bred generosity, and the Lydians secured a state of peace and prosperity never dreamed of by the royal financiers, ministers of agriculture and such. It felt like the most blessed of times, but not all shared those sentiments.

All the while, in Nathan's mind, a tiny seed of discomfort had been sprouting. What seemed to be trivial nightmares common to the overactive minds of children were in all actuality, portents of a storm that brewed deep within. His resilient childlike mind mocked the clouds that moved in upon him, and Nathan easily found solace in the arms of his parents or in cute and playful diversions. But as the child came of age, and the ways of *the boy* began to retreat within, his untended garden began to rob him of sleep. During the day, his unconscious mind, then desperately seeking to understand itself, pressed him so hard that he gave way to frequent, unexplained outbursts. His parents hoped to help by "fixing" something, either through more love and understanding, or removing some burden from his shoulders.

They found that mathematics and all manner of knots, puzzles and riddles could engross him for hours and days. Then suddenly, following the speedy onslaught of puberty, Nathan emerged from the storm. His eyes were once again bright and his fits troubled him no longer. During that transition, a toxic realization had been born in him and henceforth infected everything he had ever seen and known, as well as everything he would ever see and know; and the only trace of this infinite scorn, which he held carefully within, could be found in his clever smile. Oh, how his distinguished life seemed so petty! Nonetheless, because of his newfound resolution, he methodically applied himself to his studies and disciplines and soon outstripped his peers in every respect. Even so, after romping his opponent in a fencing bout, he would graciously offer the combatant his hand and sometimes he needed to help him to his feet. He was ready to make his mark, determined so to do with the skill of a master.

Obstitrix saw the change but didn't know what to say. He wasn't ready to alienate his nephew, so he discreetly kept his thoughts to himself. A few years passed and Nathan reached his fifteenth year. By then, his parents felt powerless and allowed the fates to play their part, for they too could see the uncanny tenacity with which their son approached the world.

Late that year, at the autumn festival, in the evening, Aretta stood blissfully watching from the castle's high northeast bridge, the Lydians who came from far and wide to feast and enjoy themselves. Looking northerly from here and over the tops of the garden trees below, the festival grounds, occupying the great lawn that stretched to the north until terminating at the sheer rock face yonder, could be seen just beyond the ascending grove of ash trees that lined the long east-west approach to the great entrance hall. Here she looked past the limestone columns that supported a network of great stone arches interwoven above. Nathan was out for a quiet evening walk about the castle. He breathed in deeply the cool evening air, savoring its intoxicating aroma. From his chambers toward the south, he had walked northwards and continued on toward the bridge. Upon entering the bridge from the southeastern archway, he caught sight of his mother. As he made his way to her, she watched him lovingly. After reaching her, she fondly wrapped her arm around him and said gently as she turned to face the gathered multitude, "I love to see them all so happy."

Nathan took a deep breath. Looking down and then away slightly, he spoke, "Are they?"

A tear rolled down Aretta's cheek and she held her son tightly. She thought for a moment and then curled her bottom lip inwardly. Releasing her grip ever so slightly she then empathetically stated what was at the source of her own tears, "You're not."

She cried as she held her son for several moments. He gently wriggled free from her grip and made his way northwards to the great reception hall where red gold-fringed curtains and tapestries and smooth marble columns and arches richly decked the walls, and nobles were gathered around boasting about their diverse achievements and good fortune.

He was a bit unnerved though as he stepped onto the gold marble floor. It seemed that at the sight of him, those present were one and all a bit startled. A fine nobleman, General Indow, sporting a monocle, which went nicely with his fluffy white beard and his stocky frame, then nicely clad with a redcoat and gold cross belts, seemed to spot him first, upon which he involuntarily spit a bit of tea into his saucer. Others pretended not to notice, while still others locked eyes upon him as he passed them by. He hardly made it halfway into the great hall when suddenly from the balcony came a loud call. It was his father, high up at the top of the white marble staircase. He called out, "Attention everyone! He's here, at last!" He motioned to the musicians gathered not far from the entrance and they struck up a tune, while the gathering began to sing their traditional birthday melody:

From life to life, new life to come;
The birth of a light, a star and a sun;
This is your day, may your glory unfold;
Light up the world, with your story untold.
Our wishes are yours, and yours are divine;
Light up the world with your wishes and rhyme!

The crowd cheered ecstatically and awaited their rising star. In Lydia, it was in the sixteenth year where a child's vocation was formally entered. Prince Nathan would now be serving his countrymen in anticipation of his ascension to the throne. Unprepared for his birthday guests, he quickly but nervously moved to the first landing of the stairs of the great hall. He began his address rather bashfully as he chose his words nervously and said, blushing, "Th-thank you. I must say … Um … thank you." He smiled widely and went on, rhythmically beginning to utter the familiar but ancient ode of their first king:

Dar, n my sond not aye;
kwikly Yid go away;
twod not fer de grond;
rich, soft dar Yi lay;
she shewed mi de way.

As he looked about the room, and the solemn look that filled the eyes of his observers caught his soul, he could say little more. "Lydians!" he said. Then he paused and reflected a little more on that look. They were little more than domestic beasts to him, trained to reverently submit to the will of the king and hold to principle as an indomitable god, in the name of law and order. They didn't know what he knew. He wondered, in their wildest thoughts, were they as pleased with life as they led on to believe? Could they not see the disease that festered deep within their souls? Or was he the only one who felt so sick of it all? "Have a blast!" he finally remarked.

Then, as he descended the stairs, he saw a young lady watching him closely, her eyes sparkling brightly with life, and deep within them he could see secret worlds turning and dancing like glistening flashes of light. He smiled cleverly at her, and she smiled back, almost giggling. She wore a shimmering purple dress and her hair drawn up high in a bun with long, thick, black curls dangling from just above her ears. Her father was the Lord of Scott's Mountain to the east, and Nathan recalled her sixteenth birthday just that summer when they swam together in her lake. As he walked on, he wondered secretly if she felt the same passion for him as he did for her; when suddenly, as he entered the darkened side vestibule to think quietly, there she stood. Tiaye had entered the vestibule by one of the several other doors, and she pressed him closely.

 "There is no life here. I was dead until I saw you just now," she whispered.

 Nathan pushed her back slightly and said, "You're just talking like a crazy kid. What makes you think that I have any life in me?"

  Her countenance turned cold and menacing. "Uhgh!" she growled as she stormed out of the room.

 No one could talk of what happened to her late that night, but it was not easily forgotten. She was nowhere to be found for all that evening, but in the early morning, a search party was sent out and soon found her body broken on the jagged rocks of the river Sheaglow, which long ago had cut a wide canyon on the western side of the castle. No one could understand what had actually happened, but the truth of the matter was that she had slipped. Yet the unsolved mystery further scandalized Nathan regarding the value and transience of life.

V

ANNA'S GEM

The following spring in Asralon, Luna was getting ready for her first job. She would be a waitress at the local tavern. "Luna," Anna begged, "finish the dishes before you leave, would you dear?"

"Mom!" Luna replied angrily. "If you don't leave me alone, I swear, I'll …"

She continued, "I'll go insane! You never let me have any fun, every little thing I have I have to work for, and you just sit there all day staring out the window, gossiping about every going on around here. 'Linda is taking her cart into the market again for her mother. Why don't you do that for me?', or 'Poor Billy is being bullied for his last bit of change.'"

"Oh, Luna, you have quite the imagination. All your life you balked and you sulked and you cussed and complained, as if your life was the only one that mattered here. When will you stop fighting with me?" replied Anna.

"Never," Luna countered as she smiled broadly.

"You are quite a spunky little girl: lively, sharp, bold, and capricious. Don't ever change," Anna lovingly concluded. "Have fun at work dear!"

"Mother?" Luna asked. "I am a little frightened. Why can't we live somewhere else, anywhere but here, the south side is so rotten?"

"Father left us this home, I couldn't bear to leave it," Anna replied. "Besides, things are the best they've ever been here, and our spirits are quite high even though we are still somewhat poor."

"Do you think the Queen will really pass through these parts today, mom?"

"Perhaps, and perhaps we'll see the new prince?"

"I'll keep a watch."

Later that day, the royal family visited the south side, during which, they showered abundant gifts upon the townsfolk. Baskets of fruit and baskets of bread, fine clothing and barrels of wine all rolled through with the royal train. The soldiers had to keep a few of the townsfolk at bay, but overall, it was rather uneventful. But neither Luna nor her mother could forget the sight of the handsome prince. He was dressed exquisitely and bore his clever grin as the wagon passed by the wooden homes and businesses, first moving south, along Broad Street, until moving west, along Market Street, thereby leaving Anna's corner home behind on their left. Reaching Bronze Way, they turned right and kept on for two more blocks. Turning right again, they entered South Street and passed the tavern on the corner where Luna worked. All the townsfolk came out to cheer and offer flowers and other accolades, until finally the procession was over. Reaching the five-point intersection adjacent to Anna's home by means of South Street, the royal party turned left and made their way northward along Broad Street, toward the King's gate.

However, just before they reached the town gate, a few scoundrels from the South Side who had gained control of the gate promptly lowered it in hopes of enclosing the royal couple in the upper town square. Their feeble attempts were instantly thwarted by the royal guard who chastised them directly and placed them under either forced service or imprisonment. The rebels arranged to spend the following weeks repairing a good number of houses along Market Street.

Nevertheless, Nathan would not soon forget the gritty scowl on the ringleader's face. His utter disregard for his father's eminence felt like a personal affront to his own authority and safety. The men were clearly insane, and Balto, the instigator, had been the subject of frequent complaints; however, never before did he do any real harm. But something had cracked. And he could often be found sitting in the gutters of the streets, muttering to himself as if he would slip away at any moment. Little did Thaddeus know, but this one peasant would soon bring him to his inevitable doom.

VI

CHANGES

Before retiring, Nathan considered the assault earlier in the day, and suddenly he realized that nothing is certain. If armed, those peasants could have killed him and his father or mother, or worse. And worse still was the utter contempt they held for his royal dignity. There was no fear in their eyes, no sense of awe or wonder: that was dangerous. 'Ugh!' he thought, 'just forget it.'

In the morning, he looked around. Any one of the guards could have killed him on the spot. And going further, why did he have to live so modestly, when he was surrounded by such wealth and authority? That day, he sat by the cliff where Tiaye fell and continued where he left off those years ago in his early adolescence. Something always felt missing, something always seemed wrong. There was a void. Life was a joke, a terrible joke; it didn't matter whether you were rich or poor, hungry or satisfied. Eventually, everything died: everything. It didn't matter whether one man rose or another man fell. All that mattered to him was that he was not the one that fell, and he reasoned to himself, "I don't have to live like this. I am the future king." And all those fools, living out their lives in mediocrity, would be easy prey it seemed. The soldiers who risked their lives defending the country from invaders were little better off than the farmers who cultivated the land. That didn't make sense. Something had to give and he would see to it.

Early that evening he sat with Obsitrix, and they talked at length about these matters.

"You know just as well as I, that in all things, there is truth. My only caution to you is that madness comes to those who try to fill a void themselves. There is another way. Acting rashly in this manner may only bring further pain upon you," the sage explained.

"Uncle," he replied, "I am in pain right now. I can't take it anymore. All my training, all my striving, it has been for this!"

"Perhaps we can discover a way. Nathan, you are a gift, there is much to ..."

Suddenly, a soldier burst into Obstitrix' antechamber and shouted excitedly, "Hurry! Thaddeus has been slain!"

Thaddeus had been walking near the river and spotted a thin and frail figure lying near the riverbank. He was bunched up and shivering from the cool waters. It was Balto lying there, helpless. He was famished and bloody. Nearby, a knife lay on the ground that was soaked with his own blood. Thaddeus drew close to examine him, and as he did, he felt a sharp object pierce the side of his neck. It was Balto's knife; he had reached for it instinctively and plunged it deep into the neck of the king and straight through his throat. Thaddeus fell to the ground instantly and was subsequently surrounded by his attending guards. First the guards, then the healers, then Aretta, and finally Obstitrix and Nathan came rushing to his side. During the shuffle, Thaddeus had motioned that the knife not be removed from his throat in order to buy some time. And Nathan, while en route, had passed Balto who, by the time the prince and his uncle drew near, was being carried off in chains; and having caught sight of him, Nathan's memories of the previous day came rushing in.

When he finally arrived at his father's side, his father's strength was nearly exhausted. Thaddeus had wanted to tell him how much he loved him, but the knife in his throat left him speechless and gurgling in his own blood. If it was removed, death would have followed forthwith. Their eyes met as he struggled to make some sign but to no avail. Thaddeus looked pathetic and quite nearly disgusting in Nathan's eyes. All the regal magnificence his father bore had vanished in this final moment. Moments later, when Thaddeus breathed his last breath, Nathan burst into violent tears. He loved his father dearly and could bear the sight no longer. His tears turned to anger, and he began to scream. Crying loudly, his thoughts turned inward to his struggle. There would be no more mercy; no more could he pretend to cherish life. Composing himself, his thoughts turned toward vengeance and retribution. But he would go far beyond that, he decided. He would invoke fear into the hearts of his subjects, and he hereby replaced his sickening hate with a scheme.

The several guards who had escorted Balto to his confinement wished to execute their prisoner at once, but all were too grief-stricken to act out their impulse. They loved their king and were consumed by their memories of his life and rule. Obstitrix soon arrived near the prison attempting to preserve order and charged the soldiers to keep Balto imprisoned for the night, so that the inquisitor and healers could see him in the morning.

But already, Nathan was executing his designs. He had determined to personally and publicly execute Balto. Assuming the capacity of king, he enlisted the help of several soldiers and vouchsafed to them on his honour.

They promptly seized Balto that very evening and dragged him down through the King's Gate and into the nearby town square. There, wagons were being packed up for the night, and torches were being lit.

The area inside the gate was laid out in a circle; and taverns, shops, and gardens formed the perimeter. Two streets originated here and meandered their way through the city: Broad, which cut its way through the city's center, and Round Street, which followed the eastern wall until terminating at the East Gate. Several rows of benches followed the interior perimeter of the square and faced a tall platform near the center. Speeches and performances were often delivered from that stage, and the entourage headed toward it. Twenty years had passed since blood had been shed in that place. When the entourage had entered through the gate, the townspeople halted in their tracks and watched in astonishment.

Nathan mounted the central platform and called out passionately to the people of Asralon: "Thaddeus, your king, is no more. Slain he was by the hand of Balto, your spawn. Never will I see royal blood spilled so freely in our land. See how it goes with the one who kills the king!"

With those words said, he gestured for Balto to be brought forward. Trembling, Nathan raised his sword and after a moment's pause, he hacked away at Balto's half-dead figure several times before striking the final blow. Balto fell to the ground and the onlookers quivered with dread. Nathan turned contemptuously from his victim, walked away with his soldiers, and left the corpse behind.

After exiting the gate, he quickly looked for a quiet place where he could let his convulsing body settle down. He made for a grove to the north of the bridge and dismissed his company. Upon entering, he became disoriented; the world around him seemed to fade into nothingness, and he became filled with dread.

After trembling violently for several moments, sometimes crying, other times laughing, he got his bearings. Blinking his eyes in disbelief, the world hadn't gone black; he was still alive, and everything appeared aright. Looking round, he felt a strange surreal clarity coupled with something dark and sinister.

After absorbing his surroundings, he began to breathe deeply; and during the next few hours, as the evening turned to dark, he fought back fears of his mother's disapproval and humiliating thoughts of outside criticism. These fears nearly consumed him. But the die was cast; he could not revert to the way things were, that much he knew. Ultimately, he determined that he would not live like a coward, and he need not pretend that he cared. He had set something in motion; and he could choose to play the vict*im*, or he could choose to play the vict*or*.

VII

DEFINED

The next morning bode ill for Nathan. Aretta was devastated on hearing of the actions of her son. She summoned Nathan to the Judgment Hall where they sat together privately in the early morning and addressed the matter in the company of two soldiers. Aretta confessed sympathetically, "I was angry too Nathan, but …"

"You would have spared that beast!" interrupted Nathan. "I did what you could never do. I acted in our best interests."

"It is not in our best interests to make an example of a mentally diseased peasant," she replied.

The years of living his parents dream began to fire him passionately, "You are willing to risk our lives, our happiness, for a diseased monster! It's time someone started thinking about US! You act like you can hold your perfect world together indefinitely, but it's only your perfect world. These soldiers here, they were with me; it's only a matter of time until they see the futility of the present state of affairs. Matters can only get worse.

"And you think it's fair to keep those who are truly gifted and talented at bay with lame promises of equality. Listen, mother, I don't want to have the same rights and privileges as everyone else, and given the opportunity …" Nathan turned toward his soldier friends and continued, "and given the opportunity, Adem, and many others would likewise reach for more!"

"The order of the seven will be meeting with us shortly to discuss your ascension to the throne. You will be barred, and Obstitrix will possibly rule in your stead. I cannot plea for you my son, I am afraid …"

"You will not be able to stop me, mother," Nathan replied angrily as he motioned for Adem and the other soldier, Galax, to come to his side. But to his embarrassment, they did not move from their posts.

"What am I to do, son? You threaten me with my own guard." Following these words, she vacillated, allowing her son an opening; Nathan subsequently seized the opportunity and fled.

He ran out of the castle, and after crossing the arched stone bridge near the springhouse, he looked back. No one pursued him.

Watching from a window, Aretta turned and said with finality, "Let him go, perhaps this is best."

Cloistered and downcast, Nathan went in the direction of the King's Gate; and upon reaching the bridge, he bumped directly into an old woman. Their eyes met, and without warning she thrust out her hand to his and gripped him fiercely. The ghastly crone turned her eyes down toward his hand, and she stared for a moment before suddenly releasing him. Their eyes met once more, and pressing her finger against his chest, she said, "Turn back now, child, a storm is brewing tonight."

He lingered for a moment before ducking to the side and walking onward and through the city gate. As he walked into the city square, he felt like an outsider, and he nervously clung to the perimeters and shadows. Slowly, he rounded the place where just last night he executed his father's murderer. The blood still stained the platform and the nearby pavement.

A storm *was* coming, and the sky slowly darkened. After passing through the square, Nathan wandered aimlessly through the city streets. Turning into tight passages and switching from one close alley to another, his mind began racing. What just happened? Was he a fugitive or an exile? What now? He strayed more deeply into the labyrinth. How would he ever make a viable attempt for the throne now that he was an outcast? He turned to berating himself for such a feeble execution of his designs and began to feel embarrassed. Few would have been impressed by such an empty bid for power, and fewer still would dare flock to his side. Even if he could come up with a scheme, his mother, beloved though she was, would be there to block the way. As he thought of his mother and her incredible discipline and control, his rage began to build. 'She had me on a leash all along. Who was I to ever dream of being free?' he ceded.

After walking aimlessly and agonizing for several hours, he rounded a corner that opened to a small grove of grey alders. A brick walk encircled the entire grove; and in the northeast corner, lay a cluster of large limestone rocks. Six wood buildings with stone foundations narrowed toward the grove and added to the air of seclusion. There was no one about, and he was frustrated and tired. So, he ducked behind the rocks; and finding a stone bench, he made himself comfortable. In a short time, he was asleep.

After about an hour, large drops of rain awakened him as they hit his face and hands. "Arrrrgh!" he muttered, as he got to his feet. By then, evening was falling, and he had nowhere to go. The rain grew steadier, so he decided to search for more suitable shelter. He walked several blocks before settling on a cluttered alley with awnings spread about this way and that. By then he was soaked; and the storm, in full tilt. There he sat on a crate he had positioned below an awning, and waited.

Night fell while he waited. The rain slowed a bit, and he heard the sound of footsteps approaching him. Not far ahead, he caught sight of a lovely figure shuffling toward him in the rain. It was a woman about his age. She was sopping wet and hurrying home.

As she drew close, he asked her politely, "Do you need any help?"

"No!" she replied with biting sarcasm.

Just then, his rage returned to him. Thoughts of his mother controlling his fate for the rest of his life sparked a fire within him. Before he could think, he reached out impulsively and violently grabbed the woman by the wrist. She promptly kicked him and quickly darted past. But it was too late. During the tussle, one thought took hold and consumed him, and that one thought overmastered him and began to dictate his every move.

Before she could slip away, she felt a firm grip on her right shoulder and a sudden jerk that knocked her backwards to the ground. The low places in the alley had filled with water, and she came down into a large puddle. She tried desperately to crawl away; but the battle was already lost, and before she could scream, a firm hand muffled her mouth. The young girl fought back with everything she had, but the beast had already begun to devour her. In those agonizing moments, the image of her assassin's face was burned into her memories. It was someone she'd seen before. Suddenly, she was released from Nathan's grip; and during the next few moments, she heard the monster's loud splashing footfalls fade into silence.

Helpless and nearly unconscious, she lay in the deepening pool. As she faded, the world around her underwent a change. A gentle presence drew near to her, and she began to feel a floating sensation in her body as if she was being suspended in midair, while the unknown visitant seemed to engulf her in a soft, tactile light. After being thoroughly transfixed, a euphonic voice possessed the air and intonated like a gentle goddess:

"Luna, you must get up. Your malefactor will go on to hurt still more; until the land is ruined and the nation mourns. Even so, in you has now been placed the seeds of change; and through this your child, peace shall be made. Rise up now and find your mother. You will find help in many places. You are my life: my bond."

Awakening, Luna rolled a quarter turn and then gathered herself together for a moment. Her eyes welled up with tears, and she felt a surging in her gut. Convulsions and vomit followed immediately. She brought herself to her knees and slowly lifted herself up. By now, the rain had stopped, but she was wet and cold. A passing stranger, seeing her struggling, came rushing to her side. At the touch of his hands, she shuddered instantaneously and nearly upset again, whereupon, she tore herself away from his cold and "savage" hands. Leaving that dark alley, she wandered the streets aimlessly for an hour before finding her mother's doorstep, and in she walked, soaked and haggard.

"Luna," said her mother nervously, "what happened?"

Holding herself in her arms, Luna slowly shuffled towards the fire that Anna had already begun to arrange and curled up in the chair nearby. Anna took a deep breath and pulling up a chair, sat near her, silent and motionless. When Luna drifted into an exhausted sleep, her mother began biting her nails and got up, pacing nervously, trying to fight back her tears.

On the following morning, when Luna awoke, she found that her mother had set biscuits and tea at the table. Moving there, Luna sat opposite her tea; and before she could drink, her memories, so fresh, pressed her severely. Sighing heavily, she pulled her elbows onto the table, and cradled her saturnine face in her upraised palms.

She poured out bitter tears, and fragments of her tragic night began to emerge through her sobs. Piecing her daughter's muffled cries together, Anna put her hand to her mouth and forcibly fought back her own tears. She cursed the good fortune that seemed assured to them when Luna was born, and found herself in much the same wretched condition she forsook that cold night when she wished for dead. Here again, she could only see life as an inescapable curse, which harshly punishes the innocent and terrorizes the poor: only a desperate optimist would dare dream of fanciful illusions of happiness, pleasantness, and fairness. She held Luna tightly and Anna's tears began to stream from her eyes. She wanted to collapse under the impossible weight of guilt she shouldered for bringing a life into such a painful world.

A painful quiet entered the home, and thereafter, a corrosive resignation took hold. Luna forgot about the sun, the joys of spring, or the days and nights of laughter with the young local girls. It wouldn't be long though, before an unexpected twist of fate would change everything.

VIII

DOWN BUT NOT OUT

Nathan, on the other hand, was boiling over. New life coursed through his being; he would return to his kingdom and break free from his mother's power at all costs. Finding his mother's illusions of propriety weak and wanting, he was determined to publicly expose the weakness of her regency as well. Only three days after leaving the castle, his plans to return were already firmly in place, but he would first have to recruit some guards from within the castle walls.

After they completed their shifts, the three guards who had helped him with Balto's execution entered into Asralon. Nathan, catching sight of them, followed them into a tavern, where the soldiers sat and started drinking. After they finished several drinks, Nathan approached his old friends: Adem, Demetrix, and Galax. "Thanks for the stab in the back, old friends," he scowled. "How did my mother reward you after such a display of loyalty?"

"We are under orders to report you to the minister of defense," stormed Galax. "You should have known that your little coup was feeble. Now get out of here before we arrest you."

"It's just a matter of time, and you'll be wishing you had supported me." Nathan replied.

"That's it," retorted Galax as he slid his stool back. "I'm taking this boy in!"

Galax reached out to grab him when suddenly three large men from inside the bar stepped in between. Adem was indecisive, and as for Demetrix, well, he was quite finished with work for *his* day. Demetrix got up and made for the door, but a fourth burly peasant cut him off. He threw his hands in the air and grumbled, "I don't need this, and I don't care about your power struggles."

Adem however was of a different mind. He once lived in Asralon like those four men. He remembered the griping and complaining that went on in the taverns among the men who felt that they worked too hard for too little. Seeing the enthusiasm of Nathan's supporters infected him. Already the seeds of grandeur that *the boy* planted in him several days ago were beginning to germinate. He felt that suddenly things could be different, that somehow, he could now have the things for which he worked so hard. "Galax," Adem shouted, "stand down! Whether you commit an act of treason against your king or your queen is not a matter to consider lightly." Seeing Galax calming himself, he continued, "Let us at least hear him out. If we're not interested, we can tell him to shove it."

"Fair enough," Galax reluctantly retorted. "But I don't see how he could ever get us anywhere."

For the last few days, Nathan had been speaking in bars and taverns in all the lower class parts of Asralon. He had enlisted a sizeable army who would die for him if it meant being free from their "miserable" lot. Many of them were moved by the lack of security that Nathan portrayed to them, and threats of foreign invasion served to anchor the fears of his audience. But hidden well below the surface, thoughts of grandeur festered in the hearts of his foremost supporters. A grandeur that they imagined was exclusive to kings and queens, noble men and women, dignitaries of state, and the chiefs of the sacred order.

Incidentally, the order was a group of men and women who possessed secret knowledge, handed down to select initiates from generation to generation. They were said to have communication with the gods and they bore sacred tattoo markings and the like.

The ancient magus Polentus was among the first to gain renown. He was credited with miracles such as the gift of moving large stones, entering the minds of his subjects, and changing times and seasons with his secret arts.

Few knew the truth as Nathan knew it, for his uncle Obstitrix had been removed from the order after attaining their highest degree of initiation. Obstitrix had blasphemously declared that "all is naught," and that even the tales of Polentus were but tales and nothing more. Dismayed, the other members of the order banded together and declared publicly that Obstitrix had become ill and that his spirit was too weak to continue in the order. That was thirty some years ago, and much of that era had been forgotten. But Nathan often saw him performing some of the sacred rites and inquired into the matter. The truth that he had discovered was that the order was powerless. Since the days of Polentus, they had long degenerated into a stewardship that merely kept the myths of the followers of Polentus barely alive, maintaining merely the guise of an "all-powerful" group of elitists.

So, following their clash in the tavern, Nathan went on to describe his current level of support and his immediate intentions; and further bribing his friends with positions of power and wealth that they had hardly dreamed of, he won them over, thereby attaining, after just three short days, a foothold on the interior of the kingdom. His mother should have known how easy it would be to overthrow a kingdom blinded by illusions of peace and equity.

One by one, many of the younger soldiers and captains rallied to Nathan's side, and the coup was set for the following week in the moments following his father's burial.

IX

THE TABLES TURN

On the day of the burial, thousands of mourners gathered at the capital. The entire populace ached from the void that Thaddeus left behind. Although people talked about Obstitrix receiving the throne, the Order was not ready to install him, and Aretta preferred to remain a widow. Besides, the popularity of Obstitrix was questionable and paled in comparison to their still-venerated youthful prince whose dark, provocative visage bore an uncanny likeness to that of his father. The queen intended to address this matter in a speech from a balcony outside the western reception hall. Following her address, she was to read an ode that Thaddeus had prepared years ago for Lydia to hear posthumously, which read as follows:

Dear Lydia;

'Tis many a year since I played in your grasses, and sang of your virtue and died in your ashes;
A wave is ascending and all that is ending, are the things that your Mothers and Fathers scarce know.

Give me this moment to rest in your bosom, and let soft earth encircle my frame.
From ashes and embers the new ways remember, until we all whisper away.
When light becomes darkness and darkness remains, in her chan'ling dithering way,

All will remember that fateful December, when the sunshine returns once again.

The burial proceeded as planned. Thaddeus was buried in the western burial ground among the kings and queens of old. The grounds occupied a hillside just above a grove of beech, fir, and alder trees. After the burial, the procession marched northward, until reaching the place where they assembled.

Five separate slate walks, bordered by several pine and fir trees, stretched out directly from a two story reception hall and formed a wide mall toward the southwest. The central walk was the widest of the five and headed toward several steps that ascended to a double portico supported by four smooth sandstone columns. From the high balcony of this immense double portico entrance to the hall, the queen would speak to the large crowd gathered in the mall below. Centered on both levels was a pair of large white arched double doors, and pairs of equally massive arched windows were set on each side. The entire western wing, which housed the reception hall, was constructed of red brick with the hall serving as a ballroom and banqueting area for parties of a more political nature; the seclusion of the western wing afforded greater comfort for their distinguished guests and was therefore best suited to the funereal mood. That morning it rained lightly, and the slate walks were glazed with an ominous sheen.

After the crowds fully assembled and the last drawls of the hauntingly melancholic alphorns faded away, Aretta began:

"Our recent tragedy burns within us all…." Tears rolled down her face followed by loud sobs from the gathered devotees.

Continuing, she explained, "our nation has lost a true and faithful friend." She paused again to compose herself. "And now, further uncertainty looms over us all. The prince has not been seen for several days, and rumors of discontent have been heard in our land..."

Suddenly, her eyes were drawn toward the large fir tree at the end of the central walk. All eyes slowly turned as they saw their prince stepping out from its cover. His timing was perfect. At the sight of him, the crowd fell speechless.

"And ... there he ... is," she said with astonishment as he slowly walked toward her. She didn't know what to think. Was this the moment she feared? Should she inexplicably demand for his arrest and risk looking like a woman gone completely mad? Or was there nothing to fear? What were his intentions? In the end, the only thing she could think to do was run away. So she turned to face the double doors to make her exit, but they were soon blocked by the guards. They swept their hand toward her indicating that she should turn and face the crowd, and that is what she did.

After traversing the entire length of the central walk with the crowds reaching out just to place their hands upon their venerated prince, Nathan reached the stoop on the lower portico. Having the advantage of such a warm position in contrast to Aretta's distant place above, he began his address: "Good people of Lydia, for many days I have grieved my father's passing. A great man, a great leader is no more.

"Lydia is still Lydia, however, and we will go on. Thaddeus has helped us enjoy years and seasons of abundance, and that need not change.

"Through every loss, however, we still gain something. A harsh reality has struck our hearts. Suddenly our mortality both as individuals and as a nation has been made clear to us. As healthy and vibrant as we can be, our way of life can never rid us of the evils that dwell deep within. Balto's crime testifies to that. We must act together to ensure our safety and security. My father will go down in history as being among the greatest kings of Lydia; yet, he had one weakness, and it proved to undermine him: he had never taken the measures that were so desperately needed. Criminals have roamed free for too long, and their victims demonstrate the clire need for stiffer measures.

"Lydia is secure now, indeed, but what will happen when invaders threaten to take away all that we've worked so hard for? How will we ensure the peace and prosperity of the entire nation for the years to come?

"Our king is dead, it is true. But the king's son stands ready to bring Lydia into a new state of prosperity and security!"

With those words, many of the attendees felt a warmth return to their heart, and contented smiles appeared on many faces: his confidence and poise was infectious. Their king was back, and he knew what they needed. Aretta could only watch as her son boldly took the kingdom without contest. How could she oppose the unalterable laws of the land? Nathan was in fact the king's son, and even if she could argue that he was unfit to rule, it was too late, now that the masses were so enamored of him. It seemed that the unalterable law of fate now triumphed.

"Attention!" the queen called out. The crowd fell silent. "At this time, we must all work together as one. We cannot let ourselves be divided, and we must not act rashly. Thaddeus believed in us, and we must never forget that. It is never possible to foresee or prevent every possible calamity; but good judgment and reverence for all life must never be compromised. Good Lydians, there are lines that your leaders would be unwise to cross, and I beg all of you to weigh carefully the words of Prince Nathan."

An air of confusion brushed over the crowd, and Nathan began to speak: "Mother, Lydia has long been a nation of wise and caring men and women. And perhaps it is my youth that causes you such reservations, but rest assured that you and father have taught me like no other teachers could. I am ready for the burdens of rule and the Lydians do well to stake their hopes on the son of

Aretta and Thaddeus! But it is true what I say, the people of Lydia have toiled year after year, and I will not see all their toil ravaged by foreign or domestic parasites. And it would only stand to reason that the son of Thaddeus could be capable of advancing the policies of his parents to even further heights. Dear Lydians, I will not let you down!"

Once again the crowd began to shout their approval as if in effort to impel Aretta to abandon her fears. He was unstoppable. In the subsequent days, Nathan forcibly argued for his coronation, which Aretta tried gently but desperately to stymie. In just three days from the foregoing speech, however, he would be crowned king.

Nathan, before even receiving the crown, got straight to work: he was after far more than just the throne. After several meetings with the diverse ministers of state, and the royal consul, Nathan formulated his plans. He found the nation's resources to be more incredible than he imagined. He quickly made good on his promises to his private guard and the other soldiers who had joined his cause. To Adem, who went on to be of invaluable and incommensurate service, he gave considerable wealth and property; and Adem quickly became his right-hand. Under his rule, his loyalists felt like they never felt before as they gave themselves over to every possibility that they could imagine.

He increased the contributions made to the poor that year and the provisions of the winter festival four-fold. His popularity increased as the year progressed, and when he doubled the nation's army, the Lydians began to see their promises of security fulfilled.

Lydia was a small land, bordered on every side by neighboring nations. All told, there were five nations that shared borders with Lydia. To the west was a maritime nation which had little interest in things besides trading and fishing. To the north and south were nations whose populace was tumultuous and fickle. The leaders constantly changed and it seemed that the masses preferred it that way. However, when it came to Lydia, all they could do was smile. Lydia was always a great place to pass through for some peace of mind, and their hospitality, second to none. But ultimately being very proud of their own land and ancestry, they had little interest in anything "Lydian": their country was so different both geographically and historically.

Much of Lydia occupied lowland plains interrupted by occasional low ranges of hills. These grasslands were situated at the foothills of a tall mountain range whose high peaks formed a crescent shaped ridge marking the western and northern frontiers. About midway along the northern border, a secondary ridge shot off toward the south before terminating abruptly into the low plains. Within that ridge, a series of eleven major peaks encircled the rolling highlands that cradled their foremost city and her outlying villages. Being the most secure place in all of Lydia, it was also the most populated. The surrounding forests and mountains provided ample wood, water, and stone, and the vast area of alpine grassland made for perfect pasture ground and farming.

The citadel, sometimes known as Mihai, extended out lengthwise from the south side of the northern summit of the same name, its rear upper corner cutting deep into the sheer rock face. In front of the castle to the east, the Great Lawn sprawled out and terminated at an ancient double-stepped wall carved into that cliff. The wall was immensely high, and nearly vertical. Directly above it was a flat where a garrison of soldiers constantly trained; the garrison served doubly as the principle recruiting station. Just beyond it, a sudden granite ridge of jagged rock ascended to the apex, Mount Mihai. Putting things into perspective, the citadel was immense, reaching a height of ten stories in some places; and the garrison on the flat, a bittock higher. The mountain peak itself towered above the garrison at a height about equal to that of the lofty wall. From the garrison, the view was unforgettable. The heart of Lydia was lush, vibrant, and beautiful.

However, since ancient times, there had been frequent raids on the eastern border. The barren flats in that direction offered little shelter for the traveling merchants. Just a two day journey east of Asralon, through the gorge near the castle and an old needle forest, the mountains gradually tapered off into barren flats. Few Lydians traveled that far, and whoever did had little options for shelter. Those flats were mostly uninhabited, and the few people who lived there were nomads and witches. True, a beastly race of disfigured giants roamed the land, but they were seldom seen. Yet, the actual eastern border terminated at the marshes and lake which lay a three day journey further from Asralon. Previous policy to avoid travel through the flats seemed to suffice; and a rare and infrequent raid on the inhabitants near the barren flats seemed little cause for alarm, but only two years prior to Nathan's coronation, a small band of raiders had reached the mountains outlying Asralon. They killed three Lydians before turning back, holding the women and children prisoner. After loading their carts with their plunder, they made their way eastward to their tribe. But they passed a small company of Lydian soldiers hidden in the cliffs, and after a battle in which ten Lydians perished, among them five soldiers, two children, and three women, the foreign survivors were captured and imprisoned by the remaining soldiers.

Not long afterward, a representative from the tribe of the nomads came to Asralon to make peace. He requested that the three surviving raiders who were also the chief's sons, be returned as a token of the peace that the messenger promised would then endure between their people. The representative's request was granted; and the captives, set free. There had been one raid since; but no one was hurt, and no one could tell whether the bandits were from among that tribe or another.

Nathan argued that such an assault was inexcusable and that tolerating such raids was obscene negligence. He further argued that opening a trade route that could make use of the eastern lake made sense; whereas fearing to travel through their own country, while paying tribute to the northern and southern nations for safe passage was ludicrous. He quickly bolstered the defenses of the eastern mountains and began to subjugate the desert nomads. For this act he was greatly applauded. Furthermore, he established a prison outside of the sight of Asralon where traitors, thieves, and threats to society could be permanently secured; yet another act which seemed rather prudent to all.

Despite these measures, the crime rate increased more and more, and the prisons became filled with enterprising brigands, seditionists, and the like. However, no one seemed to notice the correlation between the rise in crime and the rise in cupidity; the people were simply grateful that the soldiers were "providentially" there to uphold law and order.

Fewer still, could see the poison that was steadily spreading across the land. Suddenly, everyone had possessions that needed protection and one and all felt vulnerable to the whims of fate. Sharing became frightening, with proposed threats to security looming everywhere; and new threats were born from the very shadows in their hearts. Losing, whether it be house or home, brother or sister, sweater or coat, was always accompanied by thoughts of accountability. 'Who did this?' or 'This could have been prevented' and other like thoughts occupied their minds.

But that was only the beginning.

X

ARETTA'S DECLINE

Meanwhile, the Queen had long disappeared. Two days before her son's coronation she found herself wishing for dead. She had lost the kingdom, and deep inside, she knew what lay ahead. What struck her most acutely, what gnawed at her most deeply, was the fact that she could have prevented this long ago. She had no idea how painful it was going to be living with the responsibility of allowing the kingdom to be raped by her own son. But what would have become of her had she actually partook of the "forbidden" fruit? Would she have ruled Lydia with the same lofty aspirations? It didn't matter. Aretta already cast her lot; grief-stricken and laden with guilt, her wildest musings worsted her and choked out all other options.

On the eve of the coronation, what began as a plan to hide her appearance in preparation for her clandestine flight, seemed more like a morbid act of self loathing. Disgusted, she viciously gazed at herself through her tear filled eyes in her bedchamber mirror, and using a knife, pitilessly reduced the long thick locks of her flowing brown hair to nearly stubble. She further inflicted bruises and made scrape marks on her arms and legs; and across her already sullen aspect, she smeared soot and ashes. The pleasure she felt as she treated herself with such violence was strange and inebriating. After donning some ragged clothing, she slipped out of the castle through a secret passage.

She intended to travel west, to a town near the western borders, but her sketchy plans were soon altered beyond her imagination. To go west, she had to enter Asralon through the King's Gate and travel south through the city, exiting through the Sheep Gate in the southwest. Since the river Sheaglow split just north of the city and rejoined just south of it, there she would cross the river once again, traversing the west branch. From there, she would go up into the highlands until reaching the narrow, less-frequented foot pass through the southwestern ridges. This route, Purshin's Pass, was the best chance she had.

Yet, having made innumerable public appearances during her twenty-five year reign and being a woman of uncommon loveliness, escaping undetected would not be easy. Large bright eyes, perky cheeks, and soft voluptuous lips upon a kindly face and an elegant figure much akin to that of a ballerina drew many a glance; and even a momentary gaze from her blue sapphire eyes pierced clear through to the soul. And although she went partially veiled, she was all the more suspect, since few women covered their faces in those days.

After leaving the passage behind, she crept, in the dark of the night to a small boat house near the river where she waited. At sunrise, farmers, visitors and public officials began to flow in and out of the city gate, and she headed that way, concealed by the sloping hill and rhododendrons near the river. Reaching a cluster of mugo pine near the bridge, she watched and waited for a clear opportunity to emerge from her cover. With all clear, she emerged, thereupon approached the bridge sheepishly and continued onward and through the gate. When she passed the guards near the gate, they watched her quizzically but didn't appear alarmed. Upon entering the town, she drew not a few stares, but that was quite well because of her ragged costume.

After about five minutes of good fortune, her confidence built. Might she actually succeed? Going several blocks more, she approached the storefront of a local herbalist when suddenly a woman emerged. The woman crashed into Aretta and nearly knocked her on the ground; but after stepping back from the queen with a curtsy and dusting herself off, she caught a good look at her discombobulated target. "What's a lovely lady like yourself walking about so ragged?" the woman asked inquisitively.

Aretta stammered, "Mm … m … that's not your business." She turned and kept on her way.

The woman paused for a moment and said to herself, "She looks so familiar." Consequently, her curiosity was peaked and she followed her for a moment.

"Ma'am," she called out, "I hate to see a lovely lady like you in such straights. Can I help you?"

Aretta stopped for a moment but didn't turn around.

"Do you have a place to stay?" the woman added.

Aretta was about to move on but a bustle ahead of her caught her attention. There were soldiers, and they were looking for someone.

She ducked sideways into a narrow alley and leaned against the wall. After taking a deep breath and closing her eyes for just a moment to compose herself, she felt a sudden tug on her left arm. It was that nosy woman.

"This way," she said. "I can help you."

She guided Aretta to an alley that led to the back of her home, but Aretta made like she would continue on.

The woman said, "Suit yourself … But you *can* trust me."

Aretta parted ways until she caught sight of the many corners and the busy streets that lay before her. There, the painful unsettling memories of her own life's turns rushed in. Her concealed misery and deep regret began rising in her chest like a burbling spring. She looked back and saw the woman still entering her home.

In tears, Aretta called out to her, "I don't know what to do!"

The woman warmly returned to her and caught a good look at her face. Her tenderness turned to astonishment as she exclaimed, holding Aretta's face between her palms, "You are the Queen!"

XI

AND THERE WAS NO COMFORTER

All was dark. Standing at the edge of a thick forest and staring into the outer darkness, the outline of a dark hole emerged from a distant rock face. Rain began pouring down, and suddenly, to the rear, the forest edge erratically jerked closer and closer to the distant hole, every surge revealing cognitively the cavern's deep dark interior.

Lightning flashed and an obscure image appeared in the cave. With another flash, the image crystallized. A crouching leopard, with teeth bared, a wet matted fur coat, ferocious eyes, and a foaming mouth appeared for an instant and snarled fiercely. The light dissipated and all went black. Moments later, another lightning bolt lit up the sky as the creature sprang forth, tearing at his victim, now paralyzed with fear, with his claws and teeth. Flesh and blood were spattered violently about, and death was upon the leopard's helpless prey.

Suddenly, Luna awoke in a sweat. Breathing heavily, she clutched her quilted blanket. The late morning light barely pierced through her dark curtains and left her tiny room comfortably dark. She lay quietly for several moments, listening to the muffled speech and shuffling feet below, before aggressively rubbing her eyes and forcing a deep breath. With one swift burst of energy she raised her body from her narrow bed and reluctantly donned an oversized button-up linen shirt that once belonged to her father. She slipped quietly out of her room and partially descending the narrow staircase, sat just below the ceiling of the lower level, secretly watching her mother talking to a strange woman in the dimly lit room to the left.

Their tiny home consisted of two floors, the upper story was just one small bedroom with one centralized dormer tucked into the gambrel roof, which formed a low, sloping ceiling, and the lower story was only about three times the size of that upper room. The entrance to their home lay on Market Street; and from the inside, facing the street, the entry-door was on the left, and a large bow window was on the right, which offered a view of the five-point intersection nearby. Anna slept before the window, and entertained guests near the hearth opposite the entryway. Near the stairs a large preparation table held a wash basin, food, clutter, and some utensils. Aretta and Anna had entered the home through the backdoor, which led to a small storage room under the stairs. Going directly across the storage room, another low, narrow door led out from under the stairs into the main room of the apartment.

Their home was just a small part of the old inn that was parceled off into several apartments with each parcel having been purchased by an aspiring urbanite. The inn sat at the corner for nearly a hundred years before the owner finally sold due to the rapidly declining condition of the neighborhood. After the sale, the old second generation innkeeper made his living selling food and beer at a tavern he purchased several blocks north.

Luna caught the general theme of the conversation, though she could only make out a few of the key words which were spoken in more than whispers.

"What's all the secrecy about?" she blurted out.

Anna responded in her usual playful manner, "Don't you think I didn't see you there watching us all this while. C'mon, get your tea … Greenbrier sends you his greetings."

Greenbrier was the local herbalist whose actual name was Thomas, but being a lover of nature and the peculiar as well, he thought it fit to don a name that, well, practically speaking, still retained the feel of Thomas but suited his love of nature as well.

"Oh, thank God, Mother," she moaned as she rubbed her head with her fingertips, noticing how wasted she felt. "That tea has saved my life. I was beginning to feel like I should sleep for days."

Greenbrier carried a most consoling black tea that he prepared with his own concoction of various herbs and spices. His signature tea had been a mainstay in Anna's home since before Luna was born, and the warm gentle feelings that it kindled became the highlights of Luna's days of late.

"Your daughter is so lovely," Aretta stated as she came into view.

Luna was a hauntingly beautiful girl of average height with a firm body tone. Her nearly black hair flowed well past her shoulders; and though disconcerted of late, among her light bluish gray eyes, she typically bore an intense and penetrating countenance that carried a general demeanor of amiable conceit. When Aretta saw her, her unkempt hair was purposefully dangling in front of her face, partially concealing her downcast eyes and saturnine look. Still she swayed gracefully as she rounded the kitchen table, her smooth shapely legs exposed below the fringes of her shirt. With each graceful step, her elegant, shapely hips pivoted in a seamless fluid motion as they swayed left and then right. She smoothly swept up her tea from the table, and passing Aretta on her left, she sat down, folding her legs under her in the soft chair.

"Who's this?" Luna asked boldly.

Anna replied, "She is desperate and is hiding. How would you feel about keeping her for a time?"

"Who is she?" Luna remarked once again.

"I am the queen," Aretta began, "I know it may sound crazy, and a bit absurd, but …" Aretta stopped when she detected the change in Luna's countenance.

Luna began to boil violently, why she did not know, but she wished to get a hold of this ridiculous woman by the throat. She clenched her fists; and pursing her lips between her teeth, she fought back the rushing feelings.

Suddenly, the door flew open. Uncle Hal burst through the door with his usual gusto, and Luna bolted suddenly to her room.

Hal was a traveling merchant who dropped in whenever he passed through Asralon. He became famous for his unexpected yet often auspicious visits but always came bearing gifts for his beloved sister and niece. This time he had an array of dried fruits and flowers he acquired in the east. Hal had a winsome way about him, was equally daring, and consequently, didn't fear traveling even the most precarious of trade routes. His love of adventure made such exploits irresistible and gave his life pizzazz.

When he entered he was delighted to see that he had another guest to entertain with fantastic tales of his encounters with the "giants" and whatever else he could conjure up; but Luna was like a daughter to him. When he saw her disappear so suddenly, his jaw dropped in shock, and his face became pale and forlorn. It had been nearly a year since he last saw her, but this was not the girl he remembered. She was always so spirited, playful and inquisitive: trying on new and exotic articles of clothing from far off places, solving strange puzzles, tasting new and diverse foods and spices, and so on (for Luna, these experiences ultimately sparked versatile and revolutionary ways of relating to people, places, and of course, fashion). Instead, she bore a harrowing look, and her whole nature, habit, *and* hair appeared to be in complete disorder.

"What happened?" Hal appealed.

"Too much, Hal," Anna replied.

Her semblance of strength melted away. "Where were you?!" she demanded. "You could have been there!"

Anna began to walk about the room, pacing frantically.

Hal grabbed her right shoulder and pleaded, "I'm here now! Don't you see? What more do you want from me? Pull yourself together, and let's talk."

Aretta got up to leave, but something inside her urged her to stay. Perhaps her irrepressible big-hearted nature was bubbling inside her all-embracing matriarchal bosom; or perhaps it was something more, but instead of leaving, she quietly walked up the steps toward Luna's room, while Hal and Anna sorted things out.

Their voices faded slowly as Aretta ascended the stairs and as the tension between the now closely huddled siblings subsided. Aretta reached the door upstairs and knocked quietly.

"Go away," growled the voice from within.

Aretta sat down and leaned her back against the wall. Choice consoling words once effortlessly flowed from her lips; and she previously divined solutions to the most twisted dilemmas, but suddenly she felt impotent. She didn't even feel human. Moving her eyes about the room, she searched out a spark to ignite an inner flame. Instead of inspiration, every thought she found led irresistibly back to her son and flowed onward unfailingly toward her ominous nightmare sixteen years ago. She quivered with dread as her drifting mind conjured up frightening scenes of pandemic corruption and vice following her son's coronation. She stared deep into the wall for several moments before a run-away tear volunteered itself.

XII

MUM?

Earlier that morning, Nathan, readying for his coronation, received disheartening news. His mother was nowhere to be found and left little evidence of her intentions behind, excepting her signet ring and other regalia. It pained him to think that the woman who cared for him so dearly for all of his life would inexplicably abandon him at this untimely hour: so much did he long for her support. She was always so steady, so dependable; she fled from nothing, even if it meant conjuring strength from the very shadows themselves.

"Surely, she didn't think that we wouldn't work something out?" he questioned inwardly before his thoughts strayed more probingly. "Why did she try so hard to block me from assuming my father's throne? Was she just a pompous fool, too proud to see things in a different light, too attached to the old ways? Or was she planning an uprising?"

It frustrated him completely. The fresh loss of his father was tragic enough. Now his mother whom he truly loved! He didn't know whether he should search her out or have her executed. What were her intentions?

He spoke with Obstitrix at length over his concerns. But Obstitrix didn't know what to say. One thing he knew though, he would tell it *all*, now or never; for choosing silence now, possibly meant dissembling as long as his relationship would endure with his nephew.

Obstitrix gathered no lucid reason to disclose the secret visions of his mother, and once and for all closed that window to his now ruling nephew. All in all, nothing would prove to undermine the trust that endured between Nathan and his uncle. Uncle's last word of advice was quite simple: "If your mother ever returns to us, welcome her with open arms, and then you will know all that you wish to know."

With those few words, Nathan was decided. He would use his army to search her out and bring her back home safely to him.

A special unit of soldiers was immediately appointed to carry out the task. They were instructed to search nearby, and after spreading confidence among trusted captains, word of her disappearance was to be spread quietly among the more trusted ranks of his army. He didn't wish to create a tumult, since the disappearance of the king *and* queen in such a sudden manner would unnerve his supporters and diminish his authority over the now content and submissive populace. In bringing the queen back, the soldiers received explicit instructions to assure her of a safe and warm reception.

XIII

NOWHERE TO GO?

At Luna's door, Aretta wiped the wayward tear from her eyes, and after deliberating for several minutes, she, completely overcome by the sense of her own futility, fled unnoticed through the back door, and continued her journey on toward Purshin's Pass.

Meanwhile, Hal and Anna continued their exchange as Anna disclosed the matter as explicitly as she knew it. Hal held her tightly and groaned within. His original intentions were to stop for a short afternoon break before pressing on westward through the adventurous pass in the southwest. There he intended to camp with a peaceful mountain tribe who quietly roamed those parts. Instead, he resolved to stay several days more with his family in hopes of being of some support.

With Anna settled, he then made his way up the narrow stair to Luna's door. He knocked gently several times, but no one replied. So he slowly opened the door and looking in, saw Luna sprawled out on her narrow bed, flat on her belly and face, her left arm, leg, and hair dangling from her elevated mat (her sleeping mat was positioned on the long window seat that stretched across the room before the small central dormer). He quietly approached her and reached his right hand across her back, resting it on her right shoulder. With his left hand, he gently caressed her between the shoulders. Luna started a bit, and slowly rolled her left shoulder upwards to where she could see her uncle's face. Her bottom lip curled upward to a long frown, and her eyes sunk into her gloom. She forced a weak smile before speaking. "I'm sorry, uncle," she said as she sniffled, "some angel, aren't I?"

Hal wrapped his arms around her tightly as tears welled up in his eyes. His jaw began to quiver, then he held her even more closely. He breathed several times, as if beginning to speak, but a myriad of words were running through his head, and nothing felt right. After a minute or two, he could bear the silence no longer. He burst into tears as he murmured the only words he could think of, "I'm s-orry."

Hal remained with her until she dosed off one more time, after which Hal returned to Anna's side. She was preparing a noonday meal when Hal suggested, "How about I take Luna with me to the mountain tribe? She can get away; she won't have to be afraid because she'll have me, and it might do her some good."

Anna replied, "God, I wish I could get away too. Hal, that's a great idea. If only she'd be willing to go."

Anna was interrupted by Luna who had been listening at the stairs again.

"I'll go," she said confidently as she got up and trotted down the stairs.

"Luna, will you ever stop spying?" her mother said jestingly.

"Oh mother, you really are quite silly," Luna replied.

They made arrangements to leave in two days time, during which Anna was refreshed to have her brother once again at home, just like old times. Luna was rather lively herself: her excitement for the journey had her bouncing and swaggering about like she was wont to do.

XIV

LESSON ONE

Aretta, however, was crazed. Everything she ever deemed astute and congenial seemed terminally impotent, and the implications rocked her foundations. She hadn't the courage to face the truth, so she fled. Straight out of Asralon and into the wilds she went. She hadn't even given the slightest thought to either preparation or possibility.

Aimlessly she zigzagged along the treacherous Purshin Pass until she lost all sense of time and direction. She barely slept the night before, and all that first day, she didn't stop to eat or drink. The country she had traveled through consisted of low rolling hills with large patches of rich vegetation flourishing among the limestone mountain rubble that jutted out at diverse angles from the land. An occasional tree but more often a cluster of dwarf juniper, alpine rose, or mugo pine grew among the mat-grass, with sedge and small-reed growing thick near the small streams of water that trickled down from the surrounding heights. In some places, the sheer faces of the opposing mountains met and created a labyrinth of jagged fissures where there was hardly a foothold; yet in other places the field of travel widened to several hundred feet across. Eventually, the pass continued along Grey Mountain to the north and among its many twists and turns and ups and downs, an occasional cliff fell sharply to her left. Many wildflowers flecked the land, and though the pass was incredibly breathtaking, Aretta barely enjoyed it, except for a few moments on the following morning.

When night fell that first day, she huddled close to the rocks shivering and wishing for morning to come. In the morning she set out, and soon reached the edge of a thick forest, where, to her left, a stream, the Dorna, burbled out into the rocky ravine from the dark, shady wood. Suddenly, something deep within her that lay dormant for a long time awakened. Approaching a swirling pool of the nearby stream, a primeval urge welled up inside and relegated her into an autoscopic awareness of her body, now dominated by her animal instincts and lapping up the fresh sparkling water. She washed her arms and face in the clear water and felt an arcane joy well up within her. Shortly afterward, she found some fresh morels, alpine strawberries and tasty shoots of artic willow. She was especially fond of morels, and she quickly savored them all.

Shortly thereafter, she entered the thick needle forest occupying a broad soft valley that traversed the space between the southern Mount Youlden and the northern mounts, Grey Mountain and Mount Toulmad, whose joining added a deep northerly hollow to the valley. There, the mountains formed a vast basin that supported a thriving biome of old growth trees and abundant wildlife, and passage would have been easy, but something unusual happened. Aretta's delirium was reaching a new peak.

As she continued on, toward the close of the second day, a doe leaped across the path. It startled her, and as quickly as it had burst through the groundcover, it reintegrated with the forest. She nearly let the encounter pass until several steps later, she saw a straight dark path heading north in the direction that the doe had taken. It looked rather dark and foreboding, and as she began turning her head back and away from the path, she caught a glance of the doe suddenly bounding across that darkened path roughly twenty strides from where she stood.

Aretta slowly cocked her head and rolled her eyes up and to the left: she was enchanted. She could almost feel a faint drumbeat hammering away in the recesses of her mind; or perhaps that was just her heart beating a few beats faster and harder, but the drumming grew louder as she took her first step along the dark path toward the doe and then stopped when she arrived at the place where she thought the doe had bounded across. All was silent. Then, slowly the drums began to beat. Suddenly, further into the wood she saw the doe leaping gracefully across the path. This time she caught a good look and admired her stately beauty. Her light brown hue – lit by a single glorious beam of sunlight that had penetrated the canopy – beamed with a brilliant glory, and Aretta began to reminisce. She remembered those days as queen where, so recently, she felt herself dancing with love and virtue like a prima ballerina partnering with perfect grace and poise in a pas de deux. Enlivened by such splendour, she moved ahead, wishing to see that doe again and again, and as she continued pressing into the forest she continually caught tantalizingly brief glimpses. In a word, she was mesmerized by her forest friend. 'What odd behavior?' she thought.

The sun quickly faded as she blindly followed her guide over rocks and through thick evergreens and wherever the animal led her. Her exhaustion crept in with stealth, and unwittingly, she overreached even her wildest expectations of herself. She began to bound nimbly, from one place to the next, until she suddenly found herself reeling with exhaustion. By then the full moon had taken her place in the evening sky and her cool mysterious glow provided ample light here in the rocky ground near the termination of the wood. After rounding the crest of a small hill, she bent double and panted heavily. Here, the forest gave way to mountain rubble, and she looked out and saw large boulder filled clearings among the last remaining trees. One of those clearings was glowing brightly. There, in the midst of some tall circling pine, hovered a bright orb that reminded her of the sun. How she longed for his warmth, how she ached for his glow! After catching herself fainting, she mustered the last bit of strength that she had and descended toward the clearing.

Aretta had only to round the last thick pine before entering the clearing. There, she paused and took a deep breath. She felt like she was entering into heaven itself. Clockwise, she rounded the tree and began to see a circle of animals holding keen attention upon both her and the central glowing orb. She first saw a hawk perched just above a bear, next followed by a reindeer and other diverse animals, followed by a fox, a serpent, a lynx, and a vulture. Each animal seemed like a delegate to a conference meant for her. She kept watching from near the tree, as the doe emerged from the opposite side. The deer stepped forward alongside the ball of light and lay prostrate before the gathering, as if reverently worshipping these other beasts of the forest. As she lay close to the central light, her ears perked as if she began receiving some instructions. Next, the lynx approached her very slowly and circled her counterclockwise until halting on her right, near her head. The doe stretched her neck up toward the mountain peak before her, upon which the cat lowered her head and powerful gaping jaws. The doe felt the sharp teeth slowly puncture her neck; then ecstatically, she released her breath. Blood began to shoot forth and the hungry beasts dove in for the feast. Suddenly, Aretta heard wild drumming as the chaotic and bloody frenzy began to look like a dance. From the body of the doe bounded a steady stream of shadow-like does bounding and dancing ecstatically to the hard and heavy rhythm. Aretta, devoured by the energy, moved in rhyme and her body began to move wildly and uncontrollably to the beat. She thrashed her head violently about as she danced around the central light. All but that central light and the pine from which she made her entrance had faded away.

During the dance, she felt an electric life coursing through her body and began tearing her shredded clothing from her body. As her hands passionately caressed the sides of her body touching first her breasts and then gliding down toward her hips and thighs, she felt the warm light of the entire world coursing through her; and it seemed to her that the whole of creation which contained her dancing figure folded inwardly upon itself and subsequently surged upwardly like hot magma through her body.

The next morning she found herself cold and nearly naked on the bare rock of the forest floor and all was changed. No longer could she feel the inverted nature of her surroundings. Suddenly however, she felt hungry, tired, and cold. The previous night seemed like a distant memory; nonetheless, it left a deep impression. She searched out her tattered clothing and after gathering it up, dressed slowly. Halfway clothed, she paused. Again her mind had turned toward the events of the night before: she was spellbound. After dressing, she drank from the stream that flowed down between the large softly rounded boulders that were near her and quickly found some emerging ferns hidden beneath some of the nearby pines: they were delicious. Back on track, she continued her way back south toward the main trail and while en route she found a few harvestable pine nuts that fell that winter.

XV

JACKPOT

Back in Asralon, it was time for Hal and Luna to make their journey.

Hal made much of the preparations but both of the travelers bore a pack. Luna carried light, while Hal carried the brunt of the necessities. He left some of his unnecessary merchant goods behind with Anna to lighten the load. They set out that morning with Anna broadly smiling and trying to contain her pride and joy.

They made for the selfsame Purshin's Pass but before making on, stopped to visit some of Hal's friends just under a half a day's journey outside of Asralon. They lived near a small highland village whose principle trade was gem mining. Hal had met the couple, Dathan and Emilia, nearly seventeen years earlier when he was traveling through. At the time he met them, he was bubbling with excitement about the birth of his niece: at last he had a chance to show them the apple of his eye.

After resting a bit and taking a meal, Hal, not wishing to impose on his hosts, asked Luna, "Shall we continue on till dark and sleep under the stars tonight?"

But as the years go by, some things are easily forgotten, and he had almost forgotten what happened those years ago when he first met his friend Dathan.

"Before you go," Dathan interrupted, "we should talk."

"That thing you gave me, it did what you thought it would," he continued.

Hal labored to remember. After a few moments, his memory sparked. "The berry!" he exclaimed. "Well how?"

"My wife was old, and was sure to miscarry, I would have spent more time studying it but we had a need. Her life was spared Hal, spared!"

"I knew it, I try to forget that day, Dathan; of all the things I ever saw in my life … bother, I'm not on the verge of understanding it now."

"Uncle, let's stay the night," Luna chimed in.

"All right, but are you up for a vigorous climb tomorrow?"

"Let me at it," Luna exclaimed as she held up her fists.

Luna believed that she was in fact pregnant, and the thought of it made her sick. She quickly left the boys and searched out Emilia. She found her in the kitchen kneading dough. Emilia was a round old woman with a sweet rosy face and adorably curly red hair. She looked awfully cute with her blue-green blouse under a white baking apron.

After some friendly conversation, Luna said lovingly, "Sorry to hear about your loss, ma'am. Are you okay?"

"Oh, just peachy," she replied. "You never can tell what tomorrow will bring, can you?"

"True," Luna agreed. "Lucky Uncle Hal was able to help."

"Things always turn out the way they were meant to be, don't they girl."

"I suppose," Luna replied. "You don't happen to have more of those, uh…?"

"Berries … Oh yes, turns out they've been growing near our river since forever. What a curious little thing they are. I always said, 'it's nice to know that such simple things could hide themselves in plain sight.'"

"Well, I'm glad you're okay?"

"Deary," she said, "We're all okay. Just sometimes we forget it."

'What a strange old woman,' thought Luna. 'Hal's adventures must have been twice as queer as he's made them out to be.'

"Well, I can't wait to taste the bread," Luna said while she walked out the back door. "I'll be back soon, Uncle!" she hollered as if he could hear her and made her descent to the river. One thought was on her mind and she was determined to see it through.

The nearby youthful river, Yimas, had dug a gently sloping trench into the soft country land around it. She reached the muddy river bank and checked the thick brush for any signs of berries. 'Oh, I wouldn't find berries this time of year,' she thought, remembering the summer days of picking blueberries and raspberries and blackberries. And just then, she saw a thorny vine dried up from last winter tangled among the new growth. Hanging from its main stem were several dried up berries, brownish in color and curved a bit. 'Perhaps this is it,' she pondered excitedly. She took one and felt it, rolling it in her fingertips. In a moment she placed it in her mouth. It felt like those days at the temple when she received the sacred bread from the altar. She began to chew reverently and swallow.

"There you have it," she said quietly as she turned toward home and brushed her palms together. Moments later she feigned vomiting and death pangs in an attempt to amuse herself.

"Ugh," she said as she began her ascent. She had been feeling like a basket case and noticed that she was almost getting used to it.

Getting near the house, her thoughts turned toward the vibrant walk with her uncle through the gorgeous countryside that day as well as prospects of tomorrow's sights of magnificent mountain peaks and terrible chasms, which uncle had so deliciously portrayed to her during their journey. She soon was feeling content and free.

XVI

MY LITTLE YELLOW BASKET

It was dark, and the rain was hard. The thick forest gave way to a small clearing. Several strides distant stood a rocky outcropping offering shelter from the storm. Drawing nearer, a terrible and hostile presence seemed to seethe from within. A deep growl broke through the shadows and moments later lightning lit up the sky.

Driven by some paranormal goad, the prey pressed forward irresistibly; and quickened by fear, violent convulsions took hold of it, impelling the "lamb" to turn back, but it was too late. Resisting with all her might, the remaining ground was forcibly lost in three sudden bursts. Lightning flashed again, and a ferocious beast was unveiled from the shadowy depths. All went black and the beast pounced.

"Hufhhhhhhhhh," Luna took a sudden breath as she awoke from her dream. To her delight, she found herself in the calm and peaceful den of her uncle's friend. Small flames danced across the glowing embers of the nearby fire. Her soft cot felt warm and welcoming, a great deal kindlier and more luxurious than her firm sleeping mat at home. After sitting up, her stomach began feeling in knots. She paused for a moment then shook her head and shoulders. After shaking the discomfort, she moved toward the fire and transferred the few logs that lay on the hearth into the fire to keep it burning. The midnight air at their current elevation was damper and cooler than she was accustomed to back home. Luna returned to her cot, slowly pulled both her hands across her face starting at the bridge of her nose, and then wriggled her body deeper into the soft bed and blankets.

The next morning she awoke to Uncle Hal and Dathan chatting away. Emilia could be heard humming a tune as she went about preparing what smelled like was going to be a delicious breakfast. The couple had a small farm with pigs and chickens and a small herd of sheep. They had a small garden and a cold storage cellar where food was kept. Back home, bread and milk were the typical morning cuisine. The daily victuals grew duller and duller with each passing day, but this morning was exciting. Luna leaped up from her cot with an extra spring, but soon found herself pinning her arm across her stomach until the acute pain passed.

Mostly curious, she darted into the kitchen and offered her assistance.

The kitchen was a regular laboratory, with gadgets of all kinds lying about. Emilia worked at a feverish pace, as she tossed chopped potatoes, leeks, celery and garlic into the cauldron. She turned about wildly from one task to another, kneading here, chopping there, turning this and stirring that. Luna hardly began to see where she could help before Emilia called from the wash basin, "Could you get me a towel, deary? It's right there in the sideboard."

Luna quickly grabbed a towel and thrust it over to her new friend.

"Thank you, much," Emilia responded sweetly. "Now, do you think you can carry that there satchel with you on your trip?" She pointed to a canvas pack lying on the table in the corner. It was laden with all manner of dense breads wrapped in parchment along with several fresh apples. Feeling Luna's ribs she added, "I'd hate to see a lovely lady like you wasting away like you are out here in the open country."

"Sure," Luna replied as she lifted the satchel. It was roughly the size of a small book bag that she often saw professors and other more learned folk carrying about. "Thank you, you're too kind."

"Oh, it's the least I could do for a lovely lady like yourself. When I look … oh, it's silly, just the ramblings of an old woman."

"No, please, go on," Luna said. She had quickly grown rather fond of this rosy little gem.

"It's just … you're like the world, being born all over again. And in those sweet searching eyes, I see the world dancing and playing as if it were all brand new. I'll be leaving my way just like the rest of us; but when I see a young lady like you, I feel safe, knowing that life will go on and its bitter sweetness will be savored time and time again. And you, young lady, hold the stories of a thousand generations."

"Well, thanks for everything, you've been such a gracious host," Luna concluded.

"You're quite welcome … Ahh! Our breakfast is finally ready. Let's get the table ready, shall we?"

At breakfast, uncle talked about his upcoming meeting with the not too distant mountain tribe:

"They just love hearing stories of the outside world. In exchange for my stories, they offer food, shelter, and friendship, as well as the most incredible hand crafted gifts you could find. My intercourse with them is among the highlights of my journeys. Normally, I pass through, but this time, I'll be returning this way in less than ten days to take Luna back home. I hope to see you again, if I may?"

"You're welcome here anytime," Dathan replied generously.

At the mention of it, Luna began to think of home and the dreary two room hole she left behind. She began to remember the crowded streets, narrow labyrinths of alleys, and her days of school; alas, it was too much to consider, as her thoughts, tainted by a bitterness that would never fade away, drifted further than she'd hoped. Her countenance began to look dark and sullen until she paused momentarily, closed her eyes, and composed herself. She looked up at Emilia with her eyes still saddened, and paused again, closing her eyes once more. It was too much. She stood up abruptly from her seat at the table and made for the door. But as she flung open the door, a pair of soldiers stood ready to knock. They had a note in their hand and burst right in through the door and past Luna. It was an order from the king, to enter and search the homes of the Lydians for something of the utmost concern to the realm. The four friends all stood by as the soldiers stated their purpose: "We are looking for someone who has gone missing."

Moments later, they began their questioning and asked questions like: 'Are you the only ones here today?' and 'Have you seen any strangers passing through?' followed by 'Could you describe them please?' After questioning them, the soldiers apologized for the inconvenience and reassured their examinees that the matter was truly important, and then they went on their way.

Luna was too sidetracked to pay attention, but the diversion ultimately served to calm the storm brewing within her. A lively discussion about their strange encounter ensued, and after several minutes, Hal, who had been waiting for an opening, interrupted and then commenced the journey by saying, "Well, off we go! Do you have your things Luna?"

Luna left and came running back with her satchel and her pack, and Hal continued, "Very well, I can't thank the both of you enough for letting us stay the night. And what a generous breakfast! Truly, truly, thank you."

They moved toward the door and slipped out, thus beginning their journey. Dathan and Emilia came to the door and waved and shouted their goodbyes till Hal and Luna rounded the hill just a stone's throw from their front door. Just beyond the crest of the hill, the traveling duo passed an opening in the stone fence from which they could see the path winding downward to the main road below. Luna clutched Hal's arm tightly as two distant mountain peaks slowly graced the skyline. This was going to be the adventure of her life.

XVII

THE ROBIN'S NEST

After walking for about an hour, they caught sight of a young fellow walking towards them. He was dressed in raggedy brown clothing and looked like a city dweller. He was about Luna's age and made like he didn't see the two of them approaching. When they were only several strides apart, he paused on Luna's side, his eyes cast down and his form scrawny and covered with filth. As Luna walked past him, he snatched her food satchel from off her right shoulder and began to run. Before Hal could make a move, Luna had grabbed a large rock and flung it at her would-be thief.

"Give it back, you loser!" she shouted. The second rock hit him squarely in the head, and he dropped the satchel and ran off cowardly.

Luna picked up her food sack and dusted it off, after which, she felt her way through it. "That jerk smashed my pumpkin bread," she protested.

Hal smiled and rubbed his eyes. "Good shot kid!" he declared. "What a sorry attempt that was."

They both walked on for about a quarter of an hour before Hal changed his tune. The ghastly sight of the poor child had been eating at him. He sympathized, "Luna, the poor kid was starving; maybe we should have left a few morsels behind."

"Not on your life, Uncle," Luna said, "he can get his own bread."

They continued on and Luna soaked up the unforgettable scenery.

"You never can get tired of the sight," Hal said, noticing the contented joy glowing about Luna.

"It's like paradise," Luna replied.

They traveled at a brisk pace and covered a lot of ground. Nevertheless, Hal stopped several times and related some new outlandish adventure each time.

Just at the edge of the thick pine forest, Luna cramped badly. Noticing, Hal quickly rested her on a long low rock and she breathed heavily for several moments. Hal's mind unconsciously catapulted back to his attendance at Anna's bedside when Luna was born. Luna briefly caught her breath and moments later, felt something pushing. Astonished, she thrust her arm out and pushed against her uncle. After holding her arm there for a few moments and jostling her foot, she waited for her opportunity and seized it. The cramping had subsided and she ran for cover behind a thick bush.

After a few minutes, she emerged, trembling slightly. She rolled her shoulders back and took a quarter glace skyward. After one deep breath followed by a long vertical stretch, she sat down. Both of them were speechless. They sat together quietly as Hal prepared to make this an official stop. He rummaged through his sack and brought out some food, water and a blanket. Taking the blanket over to his niece, he covered her gently, and soon afterward, made a small fire. Then he began to hum a little song that he learned from his woodland friends many years back. It was sort of a lullaby and he had forgotten all but a few of the words:

Oh oh oh …   hm … hmmm … hmm … in words unspoken;
They whisper … hm …hmmm …hmm … the world's unbroken;
If   only   heard … hmm …hmmm … my bond;
Oh oh oh …   hm … hmm … hmmm … ere did I fall …
From her hand.

The long silence suddenly broke, and Luna curled her bottom lip upward between her teeth and glanced at her Uncle. "I'm alright," she said.

"I know," he said. "You're a strong young lady; I don't have to worry about you."

"I'm ready to move along, uncle," she replied after a moment of reflection.

"Let's be on our way then," he said. "Just a couple of hours and the sun will be down; by then, we should be able to reach a safe shelter that I know of in case it rains."

He looked toward the sky after he spoke. It was gray and rain looked to be in the forecast. As Luna moved on, she looked out toward the place where she had just taken cover and a show of blood could be seen lying on the rocky ground. Her mind flashed toward a time when she was playing near the city fountains with a small boy who had found a robin's nest. After snatching an egg, he ran wildly about with the blue gem in his hand until precariously climbing a large rock; struggling for purchase, he lost his grip near the top, upon which the egg came tumbling down and shattered on a rock below.

Continuing, they entered into the veil of the dark forest which was home to Hal's tribal friends.

XVIII

AN OLD ALLIANCE

In that same forest, things had settled quite a bit for the queen. During her trip to the main trail, her delirium, having fully run its course, lifted. The overbearing guilt and the maddening desperation that drove her into flight had cleared enough for her to see that her course had been guided by nothing more than outright lunacy.

Thoughts of her basic needs occupied her first of all, but as she continued walking, a sudden realization hit her. Her state was deplorable. Ripped and tattered clothing, shorn hair, and bruised and battered limbs: her appearance shocked *her*. Embarrassment and shame over the fits of insanity that she had given free reign to for several days filled her. Her practical mind was now in full tilt. She mulled over the diverse possibilities that began to open to her: return to the palace, live like an exile or a fugitive, send a message to her son or some other friend or ally, and so on. On that note, she wondered if her visions of calamity were perhaps in error, or given to her by some deviant spirit who secretly held a kingdom where he fed on the psychoses and delusions of his victims.

Whatever the case, her good sense returned to her, and she determined that the answers all lay in the hands of love. So in all matters she was determined to act with love and reverence for all. And as for the night before, which irresistibly crept into her mind accompanied by no little disgust, why that was just something she would try to forget. Her delirium embarrassed her completely, and that episode was just the crowning apex, showing where such folly and poor composure had led her.

Before she reached the main trail, she heard singing and the sound of many footsteps. In the backdrop, she could hear the slow steady beat of a deep sounding drum:

Boom ... Boom ... Boom ... Boom ... Boom ... Boom ...

It must have been the mountain tribe that lived in these parts. Steps had often been taken to ensure peace between this native tribe and her subjects, and she had spoken personally to two different chiefs during her reign. On one occasion, the chief came to the castle to personally ask that the southwest pass continue undisturbed. There had been talk of leveling the ground in several places, and building bridges to open the way for more travel in those parts, and the tribe requested assurance that their way of life continue without such interference. Thaddeus quickly added the territory from the Yimas River to a monument at the western gateway of Mounts Toulmad and Youlden to the protected national lands. He erected a monument facing the city near a passage just south of the Yimas, and he carved an epigraph into it *as well as* the monument already erected on the western side with the words:

> *To the posterity of Lydia,*
> *On this 25th of April,*
> *In the fifth year of Thaddeus-*
> *Beyond, thou seeth the land we love;*
> *Cherish it well, oh daughters and sons;*
> *By royal decree unalterable;*
> *I hereby bequeath this gift for our good,*
> *To mother earth, in perpetuitum.*

The other dispute revolved around the concern that many travelers held. It was said that this tribe committed horrifying and beastly acts: that they ate their own children and cast spells on the innocent Lydians. They were said to hold feasts in honor of the gods of lust and poison and death as well as untold other demons. Many of the reports were only partly true, but the general reaction was that having such neighbors posed a threat to the safety of Lydia; and many inhabitants from the nearby towns banded together and slaughtered a good many of their tribe. The aspiring mob lost not a few of their number as well, but an uneasy relationship continued among the Lydians and the woodland tribe to this day. Aretta and Thaddeus assured the chief, Olangbohan, of their displeasure with the violence done to the tribe and responded by setting a security outpost near the outermost town which shortly fell into disuse due to the general order which seemed to last the following years.

The tribe consisted of an earlier race of nomads who occupied much of the massif wherein Asralon then laid long before the first Lydian settlers. When the first settlers arrived, the tribe had agreed to share the land but couldn't conceive of the nature of *use* that the settlers were wont to. After seeing the first settlement in Asralon, the tribe prudently recruited volunteers from among themselves who would happily settle among the Lydians and learn their customs and ways. Consequently, over time, the Lydians became a mixed race, and an unexpected cooperative relationship ensued. Many members of the tribe, known among the Lydians as the Yimisa tribe (a word derived from the settler's perception of the tribe's ancient language), took a liking to the ways and customs of the settlers; but just as many returned to the tribe and brought with them an intimate knowledge of both the language and customs of the Lydians.

Aretta's best chance was to seek the help of the approaching Yimisa nomads. She made her way toward the drumming and followed the group closely near the rocky streambed that they followed until she could make out their disposition. Perhaps interrupting their business would have been considered rude, and she didn't want to get off on the wrong foot.

She found that the mood of the gathering was light and casual so she risked exposure. The procession halted upon seeing her and looked inquisitively. A general air of pity or astonishment seemed to occupy their faces. Just then, she remembered how much in shambles she was.

"I'm sorry friends," she openly confessed, "I didn't know where to turn."

A spokesman stepped forward and questioned firmly, "why do you come to see us?"

"Well, it was more of an accident," Aretta continued nervously. "I was planning on passing through, but I'm terribly sorry … I don't have anything … nothing."

"You are a liar and a fool," he stormed.

"I don't lie," Aretta insisted as she firmed up her posture.

"When you lie to yourself, you lie to me," he explained.

In that moment, she recognized who she was speaking to. "Chief Olangbohan?" she asked.

"It is I, oh mother of Lydia. You are in sore straights, and it is all your fault. Is that why you seek my help?" he proposed with a touch of kindness.

"More or less," Aretta stated.

"Then I will help you," he continued. "But we do not have much, and I fear that much has already been wasted on you."

Aretta was stunned. His words cut her deeply but couldn't have felt more truthful. Her prior heightened state of certainty melted away completely, revealing the scared and troubled child beneath.

"I'll try," she pleaded, as if the chief were her father or some god.

Olangbohan stared deep into her eyes as he retrieved a sacred wooden rod from a sheath beneath his vest. He turned his gaze upon it as he removed its purple cloth. Upon it was carved a host of figures: some ghastly or even horrifying, others gracious and beautiful. As he began to uncover the rod, his company bowed reverently. It was the most sacred object of the Yimisans and represented to them the whole circuit of attainment.

In the center of the cylindrical rod was carved an open eye, looking away from the rod in four directions: the eye was carved in the form of a vesica. Overall the rod measured in length about the distance along a man's arm from the extremity of his outstretched fingers to the tip of his elbow, and its girth was great enough that only a very large hand could encircle it entirely. The many pictural carvings were positioned horizontally along the length of the rod, and occupied four sides. Both of the outer points of the central eye met an orb, which, moving further away from the eye, beveled outward in a "V" to meet the general plane of the entire rod. The many images were carved using single lines creating simple yet vivid pictographs. Some images were of large heads devouring or vomiting; others were of open hands; there were swords and shields and fire, lovers in ecstasy, graphic portrayals of orgies, a head dripping with blood as a crowd below leaped joyfully, flashes of light, radiant orbs, rivers and mountains, and circles of air. And lastly, retuning toward the center, the face of the conical "V" was carved with lines hailing from the small dark orb connected to the eye. The orb was reminiscent of the black holes that members of the order kept drawings of.

The chief held the rod aloft with his left hand and staring toward the south with a look of deep love and awe, he clasped his other hand to his heart, and instructed, "Give thanks to the gods, and all we have, we will share generously."

Vivid memories of her dance the night before flooded Aretta's mind, and her body began to shake due to the uncanny semblance that this single gesture bore to the strange visions of the night before. She had never been privy to admit, but the behavior of her "primitive" neighbors had thoroughly appalled her rational mind.

Now, she stood before the chief and was obliged to pay homage to their ancient customs or possibly die of starvation; still and so, this strange ritual resonated somewhere inside. Though a little divided, she acquiesced. She lay prostrate on the ground, and in that moment of silence her own words seemed to echo through her head, 'If you do not do this, I will force it upon you.'

The chief rewrapped the rod and the tribesmen and women smiled broadly and cheered.

The march continued on to the slow beat of the drums. Aretta mingled among her new friends and felt a bit of self satisfaction for successfully joining their train. After nearly half a day of marching, they arrived at a small camp where many more greeted the company with exceeding warmth.

Aretta resolved to spend several days with the Yimisa until she gathered enough strength to journey on. She had been with the tribe nearly two whole days before Hal and Luna entered the forest.

XIX

DISQUIETING THOUGHTS

Hal and Luna stopped for the night in a rocky nook, although the rain passed them by toward the south. Luna snuggled close to Hal during the dark night, which due to the fragments of passing fog, was mysteriously comfortably harrowing.

Hal led the way all that day, making his own way through the tall shady trees and stubby understory of rhododendrons, ferns and small trees, toward a barren rocky height; from there, he claimed, he could locate his wandering friends. By late afternoon, they stood high above the forest floor on that height. In every direction they saw the forest, thickly wooded with tall ethereal evergreens; and Luna imagined the likes of elves and other woodland creatures dwelling right there under the canopy.

True to form, Hal spotted what seemed to him like a small camp of Yimisa not more than a few miles from their location. He called out to them with a high rolling call saying, "Aiya, Aiya, Aiya, Aiya!" The call was soon returned with a faint sound of the like.

The pair made their way down and traveled westerly, in the direction of the camp. After about two hours of walking, a pair of scouts found them and led them straight to the camp which was just a short march northwesterly. The camp was situated at the fringes of a field of boulders. Several fir trees and a few low bushes dotted the field, and a prominent rock rose not far from the camp to nearly the height of the trees.

Night was falling fast, so after entering their yuranga, they quickly laid their packs down and prepared their beds for the night. Afterward, Luna emerged from her tent, bearing her satchel of Emilia's bread. Pulling out a loaf, she offered some to the Yimisa who were about to share their evening meal with her and her uncle. Uncle emerged with his mouth harp, and placed it in his upper pocket for circle time after dinner.

While on the road, he had warned Luna that the Yimisa were very keen people; and every night, they gathered about a fire to share stories and chant. They were very free with their feelings and used such times to speak candidly about whatever was on their mind. His main caution to her was that if ever they strayed into difficult matters, it was not considered rude to take one's leave.

After dinner, Uncle Hal began to play a quiet and mellow tune. A few of the hunters told stories of the places they went during their hunt that day, while a middle-aged woman with long black hair and prominent front teeth moved close to Luna. She grabbed Luna's hand and looked inquisitively. Luna looked at Hal who pursed his lips together and raised his eyes. Luna courageously held her place. After several moments, the woman asked, "Are you pregnant?"

Luna replied with a bit of reservation, "no?"

"Your child will be the son of a nobleman and will rule his people with great balance ... He will have to endure a trial."

"That's not possible," Luna replied angrily.

Looking closer, the woman perked up, "Oh! But you shall strike fate in her heart; and you will live willfully ... but you are not prepared."

Luna turned away and asked her uncle if they could leave.

"I'm sorry; I'll take you to our tent. We can leave in the morning," Hal suggested.

But Luna wanted to leave now. She felt something bursting from within that she didn't have the power to stop.

"I can't, Uncle," she went on. "I never should have come with you!"

"I should have known," he confessed. "I wanted to see that light in your eyes again so badly, that I didn't realize what could happen."

"Well, you should have known that I'm half dead already!" she screamed as she backed toward the tent. "You can just finish me off; I'm sick of pretending that my life isn't ruined ... Sick of it!"

Luna ducked into the tent, huffing angrily. Hal followed close behind. After he entered, the fifteen or so who were gathered there outside the tent began to chant in unison at the middle-aged woman's direction:

Ooohu hum ... Ooohu hum ... Ooohu hum ...

The sound felt like an invitation for a god to enter into their circle. Drums began to beat militantly, like rolling thunder, and the rapid pounding rhythms gave an irresistible charge to the evocation. Feeling the rhythms calling to her from deep inside, Luna turned and looked toward the circle with a fiery look of intensity. A sense of invincibility overcame her along with the desire to tear something to pieces. Suddenly, she sprang from her crouching position toward the door of the tent, walked outside, and took her place among the company: trembling. She seated herself in a central position among the group, and crossing her legs, held a strong upright posture. A young lady approached her and attended to her for over an hour to guide her into a trance.

Luna's inner eye began to open and she could sense herself seated in front of the fire with indefatigable poise. Slowly, in the periphery, several figures appeared, dancing a sort of war dance around the fire with large various-colored masks. Their aspects were somewhat menacing and sinister, yet colorful and innocent. They pranced about mirthfully with their own eternally immutable expressions conceitedly flaunting their own representation of some recondite truth.

Eventually, the central fire arrested her attention until the sight reached the verge of unhinging her. Just then, the malefic energy that had been boiling in the fire exploded in a sudden burst! A pale-white chiseled face rose from the flames and laughed at her menacingly, "Ha, ha, ha, ha, ha, ha, ha, ha!"

The laugh rang out and echoed in her head as her body trembled and her lips quivered. "No!" she cried from somewhere deep inside. "I don't want to see anymore."

But seized by her own tenacity, she firmed up. She continued watching, as slowly, a pair of lovely dancing figures ascended from the flames and began a counterclockwise journey about the fire. Up and down and slowly twirling, the pair, decked in elegant, white finery moved in the dark void around her. They looked like toy figures locked in a dance frame, and as they neared her, she grew more and more spellbound by the perfect wavelike rhythm of their course. Floating across her view, she looked hard and pulled images of their faces to her mind. To her wonderment, she saw *herself* dancing with *the prince*, Nathan! At the sight of it, a fit of hysterical cachinnation seized upon Luna, upon which the drumming gradually subsided and the chanting ended. Luna's attendant eased her out of her trance, and Luna emerged quiet and subdued.

Her first lucid memories were of her companions hugging her one by one, followed by Hal helping her to her feet to take her to her bed. In her dreamy state, Luna was quickly and easily overtaken by sleep. After laying her down, Hal quietly tiptoed out from the tent and continued on with his friends for several hours, talking about his adventures and showing them some of the bizarre trinkets he had discovered in his travels.

Luna however, tossed and turned for many hours. Repeatedly she had that dream about the ferocious leopard tearing her to shreds. Over and over, she confronted the beast, each time with a slightly different attitude; yet every encounter yielded the same results: the beast leaped forth from its place and devoured her. Beast, terror, defeat: the sequence repeated with unerring predictability. But something had changed. She was lucid and knew what to expect. Each time the dream began, she had the courage to prepare herself for the gruesome climax. The finale to the dream began to wear on her, in much the same way that one's patience is wearied by continually failing to grasp an object lodged in a crevice, just out of reach, every attempt spinning or twisting the object or worse still moving it further from one's grasp. Eventually, she simply found an insatiable anger mounting in her, propelling her onward.

As the night wore on, she simply wished the morning would come; or she'd simply rise from her resting place and get on with the day, but something kept her fixed upon the dream: she didn't want to quit.

Morning came, and the dreams had long faded into an incoherent blur. Nothing but scattered memories remained, accompanied by strange fascinations with certain orderly geometrical figures and quirky rhythmic mental exercises that involved some sort of repetition and were reminiscent of the undoing of a lock. She was nevertheless rested and ready for the day ahead.

One thing of the previous night did stick with her though. Her trance brought her face to face with that which fear bound so deep within her. She was attacked, and she remembered the attacker. An intense anger burned within: reckoning with the truth brought its own storm clouds. It would almost have felt better to live in partial denial, half dead with a half believable hope: previously, at least she could sort of cling to an illusion of purity and innocence by means of a denial of the attack and the accompanying forceful stripping thereof. She wanted to scream, to throw something, to knock someone out, anything to relieve the feeling that was nearly bursting from her soul!

"I'll kill him! I'll kill him!" she gritted as she muttered within. She clenched her fists tightly and took a deep angry breath. "It's hopeless!" she concluded. Finding no outlet for her anger, it threatened to transform into despair, if not for her young lady attendant from the night before, Ilana, who, noticing her anguish, approached her side and attempted to comfort her.

Ilana was a young petite woman in her early twenties. She had long straight black hair and a friendly and pretty smile. Luna was clutching her knees as she sat crouched, low to the earth, near some small boulders just outside of her tent. Ilana had come close to her and reaching with her arm, extended it around Luna's shoulders. With a sudden jerk, Luna turned a cold shoulder, and Ilana retracted her arm. She sat there puzzled for a moment until her eye caught a glimmer from Luna's neck. There, from a thin, black leather cord, dangled a silver pendant with a pearl setting. In a flash she grasped the necklace and tore it away from Luna's neck; before Luna could react, she sprang to her feet and gave Luna a shove, following which Luna landed on her bottom. Ilana took off in a sprint, and after putting enough distance between her and Luna, she turned back tauntingly, dangling the necklace and wagging.

If it were not for the fact that that pearl was one of her few cherished heirlooms that served as a token of the memory of her unknown father, she may have simply thrown a tantrum or made some other gesture in disgust; but instead, she bit into the charade. She sprang to her feet in a rage and clenched her fists tightly: the chase was on! Hurdling over rocks and boulders, she pursued her antagonist out into the nearby field of boulders. After running a short distance, Ilana quickly scaled to the top of the great rock-mass in the center of the field, reaching the top as soon as Luna arrived.

"Ahhhhgh!" she cried out in disgust as Ilana stood at the top smiling triumphantly.

Luna thought for a moment and suddenly turned back toward the camp, running. By now the Yimisa who sat gathered around the morning fire, enjoying hot drinks and the cool morning air, watched the antics of the two girls in amusement. Luna headed straight for Ilana's yuranga, and ducking inside began tossing item after item violently through the air and onto the rocks outside. It was more than Ilana had bargained for. She quickly made her descent and rushed over to her tent. Luna was holding a small booklet and a pair of undergarments as Ilana arrived. Their arms locked as Ilana grabbed both of Luna's wrists. Feet planted firmly on the ground, they stood opposite one another as Ilana pushed against her with all her might and wrested the booklet and the underwear from Luna's hands. Luna gave Ilana a firm kick, and Ilana stumbled backward and landed on a large rock. Luna reached for the ground and grabbed a small stone, about the size of a man's fist and clutched it with her fingertips. She swung her hand down firmly against Ilana's head, striking her roughly, just above her right eye. Luna nearly brought the stone down to deliver a second blow until she saw the blood beginning to flow from the first wound. She dropped the stone and brought her hand to her mouth. Aghast, her eyes widened, and by then many of the Yimisa had approached to help. She looked around at the tribe who mostly stared inquisitively at the two girls. An elderly woman stepped forward to care for her injured friend.

"Oh my God," Luna gasped. "I'm soo sor-ry."

Moments later, Ilana, coming to her senses, brought the back of her hand to her forehead, after which she lowered her hand and gazed peevishly at the blood. She shook her head gently, while with her lips pursed she squinted and took a deep in-breath. As she caught sight of her abashed attacker, the corners of her grimacing lips gradually turned upward. She couldn't contain her laughter any longer, which burst suddenly through her nose.

Luna, who the whole time watched nervously, let out a sigh of relief. She chuckled joyfully before cradling her face in her palms and taking a deep breath.

"You jerk," she said suddenly, "what was that all about?" Not expecting a reply, she extended her hand to Ilana and helped her to her feet, and then the two girls walked off together away from the crowd.

"Here is your necklace," Ilana said gently as she returned it to Luna's neck, "I'm sorry, I just couldn't see you … so … so hurt. You have to take it slow. And don't give up." Tears welled up in Ilana's eyes as she finished speaking.

Luna hugged her tightly and said, "I don't think I'll ever feel 'normal.'"

"Don't give up," Ilana repeated, "just don't give up."

"I won't," Luna replied solemnly.

The girls turned to smile at the gathered onlookers, and the day continued on with relative normalcy.

About an hour after the tumult, an elderly Yimisa hunter gave a loud cry. In moments, the whole company began packing up their tents and belongings. They were preparing to meet with the rest of the tribe and needed to travel the rest of the day to make camp in time.

XX

THE MISFIT

The company traveled through the old forest by following a meandering path that crossed many small streams and burbling springs. The forest floor was covered with a springy, dense soft mat of pine needles, moss, and cones: it almost felt like walking on air. The reddish brown color of the fallen needles felt warm and rejuvenating. Walking for such long hours at first seemed like it would be dull and laborious, but for Luna it soon felt like she was being whisked far, far away from the harsh and all too familiar realities of life. She let her spirit soar, and the cool clean air brought vibrancy to her face.

Aretta had been fully refreshed after her stay with her Yimisa hosts, who generously shared all, including clothing, and prepared to leave the following day. She had plans of continuing on her original course; and upon emerging from the southwest gate, she would head for the road, Great Bottom Loop, which lay near the foothills of the mountains on the western side. She would take the loop eastward until she reached the abode of her loyal long-time friend, Ellen. The three-day journey involved descending through the forest and after reaching the foothills of the mountains, it crossed serene virgin grass plains. Except for a few small farms and one abandoned military post whose main interest was in maintaining the road during the summer months, the road would be quiet and undisturbed. At Ellen's, she could safely wait until she ascertained whether it would be wise to return to Asralon or not. She could even write to her son and reopen the lines of communication if that seemed prudent.

During her stay, Aretta had quickly become a favorite of the Yimisa children. They all gathered around her, taking turns playing games and telling stories; the children jumped into her lap and soaked up her warm love and affection. To them, she seemed like one of the angels from the stories that their parents sometimes told.

Her Yimisa sisters found Aretta's industriousness indispensable, and they too naturally inclined towards her when they needed a listening ear. Aretta truly had a magnetism that was hard to ignore. It was no wonder that her subjects felt so content and at ease with her as queen; she had such a tender and gentle way and could quickly win the trust of even the most hardened soul.

When the hunting party returned that evening, dusk was falling, and the sky was crystal clear. Around the several circles of fires, the tribe could be seen gathering and settling in their diverse camps for the night. An empty circle was already prepared for the arriving party, and the chief waited there eagerly while the train headed his way. This evening he would join with their circle and they would discuss the events of the last few days. The travelers slowly made their way toward him, and after being greeted one by one by Chief Olangbohan's broad smile and strong warm embrace, they began setting up their camp rather efficiently.

When Hal crossed his path, the chief's countenance lit brightly.

"Hey, old friend," he exclaimed as he offered his arm to Hal. They kissed each other on the cheek and the chief continued speaking until his eyes met Luna, who approached Hal's side looking a little downcast and insulated.

"This must be Luna.… What an incredible girl she is! This, the whole of woman in her entirety, embodied, right here, before my eyes." As he finished his eulogy, Luna slowly looked up toward her admirer. She had been thinking as soon as she drew near to the camp, 'What now?'; but chief Olangbohan's words quickly assured her that the natives didn't all lack charm. Perhaps the evening could progress rather "normally" and she could get some reprieve from their preoccupation with causing a scene. 'Still a rather odd way to be addressed,' she admitted to herself, as she cast her eyes downward and pretended not to notice.

"Lucky indeed," he declared as he patted Hal firmly on the back.

Hal brought Luna and their belongings into their appointed yuranga and noticing her reservation, said gently, "Are you ready?"

Luna responded with a little sarcasm, "For what?"

"You're not…. Okay. I'm just trying to make sure you're comfortable, and you know, it's like I said, 'You never can tell what will happen.'"

"Great," Luna continued. "I think I'll just take a walk." She got up and walked about the fringes of the camp looking at the star studded sky in wonder. She thought of all the stories that people told about the wild creatures and personages who could be traced among the stars. 'What a bizarre congregation they make,' she thought. She lowered her eyes slightly and looked about in wonder at the rocky heights that surrounded her and stood between her and the edge of the universe. The camp was nestled in a ring of rocky ridges that circled them in every direction but southwest. Her eyes turned toward the distant fires; and she watched the happy families and friends who were laughing and playing near the fires and soon caught herself longing not to feel like such an outsider.

But she was. In fact, she always was, it was only lately that she suddenly cared. It was always just her and her mom against the world. Sure she had uncle Hal, but he was just an added bonus that, on occasion, spiced things up a bit. She never before tried to fit in or belong; but suddenly she wanted someone who could reassure her that she was still alright, and yet how could anyone ever like her now that she behaved like a freak who constantly

Mark J Graver

needed something or was ready to break down at the slightest disturbance? She continued watching, now troubled, as across the field, a gracious womanly figure sat as a child came in close for an embrace. How she longed to be strong and kind like that woman. But that was not her mother. Her mother was always working or complaining and rarely shared her affection. 'It's no wonder I'm such a loser,' Luna thought, 'just a hard little girl from the slums.'

She returned to the camp hearing laughter and singing. Disgusted, Luna shut herself in her tent and quickly tried to curl up in her bedding; she desperately wanted to go to sleep and forget it all. After tossing and turning for several moments, someone entered the tent. It was Ilana, who came in to see if she wanted to take a walk. Luna shuffled a little under her blankets, pretending not to have heard, until reluctantly rising from her bed: sleep felt like a much more frustrating prospect anyway.

They wandered away from the camp toward the gentle noise of a spring gurgling below the rocks. Ilana began describing her life growing up in the wood. "I think this is my favorite part of the forest," she said. "We've come here time and again growing up. There's a beautiful lake here and it's great for swimming. In the winter, the lake freezes and is so much fun, but once when I was little, a boy went out too soon and fell under the water. The chief was close and ran out after him. The ice cracked and the chief crashed through. After a long pause, the chief emerged far out near where the boy, Pogo, fell. He had the boy in his arms and many of us worked together to get them both out. That was so crazy!

"Oh, and I love the sheltered, cozy feel of the surrounding rocks. We climb them all the time, and look out toward the distant plains. I wish to fly like the eagle and soar over those plains.

"Did you know we could see Asralon from here? There is one peak where we can get high enough to see through some of the distant mountaintops, and there it is, like a little dot, way off in the distance. Hey, I bet sometimes I was looking right at you and didn't know it."

As she spoke, the firelight that filtered through the trees grew dimmer and dimmer; and on the forest floor, faint patches of moonlight lit the ground. Suddenly, an eerie chill came from the pit of Luna's stomach: they were all alone in the dark. They continued walking together until they heard footsteps quickly shuffling through the fallen needles and leaves. The rustling grew louder and louder, until a voice called out, "Hey, wait for us!"

It was a small group of young Yimisa boys and girls, their ages falling near Luna's and Ilana's.

"Want to have a chase?" proposed a voice from one of the shadowy girls.

"What do you think, Luna?" Ilana asked.

Luna hesitated, but an urge for adventure prevailed. "Sure," she replied, "catch me if you can!"

Luna ran off into the dark and ducked behind some thick shrubs. She tried to control her panting as she crouched in the dark shadows. She listened to the footsteps scattering in every direction. Then suddenly, "Gotcha!" a young girl cried excitedly as she sneaked up behind her. For about a quarter of an hour, the children ran this way and that, ducking behind trees and rocks and finding many an unusual hiding place. They generally stuck close together and regrouped from time to time to see if anyone was left to capture. Luna kept the chase close to the stream; she found its mysterious noise most enchanting – and comforting too.

After they were through, they sat together under the stars in a small clearing created by a small ring of tall rocks. They talked wildly and excitedly for about an hour about the fun they had and the adventures they hoped to go on that summer before everyone returned to the camp to retire for the night. All sense of not belonging had momentarily vanished from Luna, and she rested quite comfortably.

XXI

WHAT TO DO?

It had only been four days since Luna left Asralon, and Anna was already feeling the void. She had cleaned the house roughly twenty-six times, and rearranged the mantle about thirty times as much.

She had made a living mending shoes and garments for her neighbors. She couldn't bear to charge much, but did excellent work. Sometimes she had little to do, whereas other times she worked around the clock. Outside of that, she went out to clean for her cousin's widow Sarah once every week, and in return, Sarah gave her enough money to go to the market and buy bread and cheese for the both of them for the week.

When Anna returned home from her errands with Luna now gone, she found the empty home a bit unsettling. She understood that Luna was growing up and would leave soon, but not having her around those four days brought the reality of an empty home too near for her comfort. She reminisced of the happy times she had shared with her cherished daughter. Luna was like a lamp that warmly lighted their little home and brought meaning to her life. Anna was not ready to live without Luna, and she didn't think she ever could be. She felt like the luckiest mother in the world to have had such a lovely child.

There were so many times when Anna wished she could hold her daughter in her arms, but life had taught Anna a different lesson. Everything could change in an instant, and a woman who was unprepared for the shocking truth would be swallowed whole. This meant that Luna had to learn to be an independent woman, as her mother had learned to be. Many times Luna begged for her mother to intervene in some difficult matter; but time and again, Anna gritted her teeth patiently and held her peace while the child searched herself for answers. Luna never failed to astound her mother as she seemed to create miracles out of thin air. She proudly held Luna close at those times, congratulating her daughter for her ingenuity and wit. Consequently, Luna quickly became quite bossy and rude, although she had a sweetness and big-heartedness that no one could mistake. Nevertheless, Luna was Anna's gift; and Anna was determined to present her gift, unspoiled, to the world.

Her world had lately grown colder and darker, and little did she know of the dangers that awaited the poor unsuspecting people of Lydia. Rumors of unrest began to circle however, with the queen not making any public appearances for nearly a week; yet the new king kept his subjects busied with many projects, and slowly introduced to them a faster, flashier pace of life, thereby giving them new dreams to dream.

And yet, more and more, reports and logistics were gathered to Nathan, as he began to assess the kingdom he inherited with keen precision and a desire intent on making a world after his own fashion.

XXII

WHAT HAVE I DONE?

The next morning, the camp was bustling with activity, and Hal was making his final preparations to leave.

"I have to get her back home," he said. "Her mother has never been apart from her for more than a quarter of a day. I could see her now, pacing wildly at home, moving things about from place to place, fanning herself, muttering my name under every breath and wagging her head."

The old chief who was standing by frowned congenially.

"I may be back through, but I have a certain sick feeling in my stomach that I can't explain. I've never struggled so hard to plan ahead."

"I know," the chief replied, "I fear our years of peace are drawing to a close.

"Hal, please excuse me, I'll speak with you again shortly before you go." The chief departed and drew near to the camp where Aretta was staying. He came over to the entrance of her tent and the two of them began talking.

Luna had followed the chief with her eyes as he went, and when Aretta emerged from her tent, she blurted out, "Hal, that's the queen … she was at our house!"

Hal slowly looked over, and Luna stared in bewilderment. Her confusion turned to anger, as the monstrous memories of the prince rushed into her mind. Luna irresistibly moved closer and closer to the queen at a steady deliberate pace. Her anger concealed, she channeled it deep into her solar plexus. As she pursed her lips together tightly, her expression soon became bold and fuming.

She didn't know what she was going to do, but something drove her on as if she was being pushed from behind. The queen was standing with her own tent just behind her and to her right, and the chief stood opposite, facing her. Luna rushed steadily toward her on her left flank. As she drew near to about five paces away, Aretta caught sight of her and became startled a bit before taking a step back toward her tent and facing her pursuer.

Five, four: Luna's hands at her sides opened menacingly as she closed in, and tears broke through her cold expression. Three, two: she quickened her pace and reached for the queen. One … she grabbed hold of her prey, her eyes filled with tears.

"You bitch!" she shouted as the queen was forced backward into the wall of her tent. She began to scratch and tear at her and pounded her fists against the queen's breast. Luna's tears poured down her cheeks as her pounding fists gradually grinded to a halt.

"Ahhhhhghhhh!" she screamed angrily.

Aretta had offered only gentle resistance. Her unquestionable innocence shone through like that of a scapegoat. But no, Aretta could not feign innocence in this case; her beastly son was testimony to the evil craft that must have secretly poisoned her wretched family. No, indeed, Luna had the villain in her grasp.

But her anger had already begun to subside. This was not her attacker. No matter what she wished, she would not get justice from this fight. Frustrated, she pushed the queen back and turned away.

Aretta quickly came to Luna's side. She wrapped her arm around Luna which Luna uneasily accepted. "I am so sorry," she said sincerely.

Luna began to feel the depth of the queen's empathy; it was like nothing she had ever felt before. It was comforting and winsome. Luna shuddered with resistance. But Aretta mirrored her feelings so perfectly that soon the two were locked in an embrace and were crying profusely. Luna had never known a love that was so warm and accommodating. Perhaps it was the queen's age, iconic status or maybe something beyond her understanding; but Aretta felt like a mother to her.

Luna composed herself and swallowed her tears. She put an arm's length between them and looked across at her queen and into her deep blue eyes. Her tears trickled forth slowly, as she began speaking. There, she openly told everything, and as she drew to a close, Aretta could hardly stand. 'Luna has every right to be angry,' she thought. 'What have I done?'

Aretta felt sick and crushed by the weight of responsibility that she carried, for she now felt certain that the angel had spoken for the good of all. She couldn't bear the thought any longer and ran back into her tent, sobbing; but Luna was not ready to let matters rest. Frustrated by the queen's silence, she followed her into the tent.

"What do you have to say?" she said as she entered.

"I'm sorry," Aretta repeated gently, "I'm sorry. This never should have happened."

"Well it did," Luna insisted, "Is that all?" She waited a short moment for a response.

"Ughh! Why do I even bother?" she continued. "This is disgusting."

Aretta suddenly felt a surge of inspiration. "I know," she replied while wiping the tears from her own eyes, "that's why I'm running. Terrible things are happening Luna; I wish he had never been born. *Anna* is your mother, right?" She remembered their brief encounter, and Luna nodded. "Can you bring her here?"

"Why," Luna returned, "you didn't screw our lives up enough yet?"

"I can take her away from the city; we could live in the country. You'd never have to return. It's not safe anymore. I have some friends who live in an isolated place. It's actually a castle, but it will be safe. You can come there with me and bring your mother too. Maybe, you have some other friends or relations who you'd like to bring as well?"

"No," Luna replied, "just my uncle, Hal."

Hal, who had come near to watch over his niece stepped forward. "That's quite alright, ma'am," he said, "I prefer not to settle down, keeps me young; but if what you say is true, I'd be the one to get Anna. She'd listen to me, and I wouldn't have it any other way. Besides, I've always wanted more for her; she's such a treasure."

Luna thought for a moment and though she didn't want to go back home to the filthy narrow streets and dark memories, living with the queen seemed like a recipe for disaster. It seemed, her only options were to stay here or to go with the queen. 'I bet I could really learn to like it here,' she thought as she reflected on the light and airy feeling that abode with her in those forests, 'and I'd hate to leave Ilana.' But she was already far too domesticated. And visiting was one thing, but staying was quite another, with winters and rainstorms and all. Besides, living at a castle was a tempting prospect, but then living at a castle with her mother made that look like a chore too. Nevertheless, she reluctantly admitted, there was something about the queen that really touched her. But though the balances weighed in favor of the queen, she probably didn't have much say in the matter anyway. So when Hal asked her, "What do you think, dear?", she replied solemnly, "I guess I'll go to the castle."

Hal made arrangements to leave Luna behind and meet up again in about ten day's time. Luna was ecstatic. "Yes!" she exclaimed as she looked toward her Yimisa friends. "I get to sta-ay!"

XXIII

A NEW WAY

Three days after Aretta had fled the royal palace, General Indow, a longtime clandestine opponent of Thaddeus' national forest preservation policy, and an even more vehement opponent of the toleration of Yimisa nomads, took advantage of the vacuum created by Aretta's absence and gave the new king disturbing reports of threats posed by the Yimisa people. The king promptly sent a company of soldiers who were ordered to carry out a charge to ensure the safety of the nearby settlers. Their first order was to investigate the truthfulness of the said claims, and if necessary, bring to justice the perpetrators of such crimes.

The soldiers made their way southward and reached the outlying towns where several attacks were purportedly made. They found little evidence of the unscrupulous advisor's claims. They, however, proceeded onward into the protected lands to locate the tribe and speak to them personally. The scouts entered the forest at approximately the same time that Hal left for Asralon.

Late in the evening that day, Hal caught sight of five armed soldiers making their way through the forest. He quietly attempted to pass them by, but was quickly blocked and questioned. Pretending like he was just passing through, the soldiers stepped aside and wished him well, but Hal didn't like the feel of it. He didn't fear for his friends too greatly, however, knowing that an act of aggression from so small a company was just suicide; but his sense of urgency heightened. Never had he seen soldiers in these parts before. He hurriedly made his way into town to retrieve his sister, and after much grumbling on the part of Anna and ten days later, he returned to the tribe with his sister reluctantly following.

During the first part of those ten days, Luna kept a watchful distance from Aretta, but as she continually saw her gentleness, and the love that the tribe felt for her, she began to long for her company. Ilana and the other girls kept her occupied for most of the time though. They spent most of the days and nights dancing, rock climbing, swimming (a skill, which Luna hadn't acquired in her youth, but nonetheless quickly mastered), and laughing. Luna was having the time of her life.

Chief Olangbohan had a few surprises though, especially when news of the approaching soldiers reached him. Before they arrived, Luna and Aretta were taken away together from the camp for the day (the chief purposely sent them with a guide who couldn't speak their language); and along the way, the two formed a friendship that would last the rest of their lives.

Back at the camp the chief handled the matter expediently and also sent a pair of delegates, bearing a gift for the new king, to assure him of their peaceful disposition. All in all, except for their preparations for their annual May festival, which occurred on the ninth day after Hal's departure, the tribe at large lived happily and without a care.

When the day of the festival arrived, everyone had something special prepared. The queen had prepared to address the whole assembly with a ballad. Near the lake, the entire tribe gathered to celebrate. As the sun sank low on the horizon, Aretta, dressed in a fine white flowing dress borrowed from her Yimisa "sisters", ascended a rock, from which she would easily be heard. The assembly fell silent as Aretta began:

Flowing; gently flowing; trickling down from the ethereal height.
Going; fondly going; searching out every world hidden from sight.

Floating; swiftly floating; like the dew as it kisses each face with light.

> *You are in the stars; you are in the stars; tonight!*
> *You are in my heart; you are in my heart; tonight!*

Throwing; wildly throwing; myself: body, heart and soul into your arms.
Evil; breathless evil; stand at attention, come the venom that charms.
Burning; sudden burning; courses through my veins, tenderly she disarms.

> *Intoxicate me; alleviate me; tonight!*
> *Moving near to me; suddenly I am; breathless!*

Filling; she is filling; the emptiness, loneliness, icy inside.
Stilling; she is stilling; all of the tempestuous fierce flowing tide.
'Twas Washing; fiercely washing; sacred memories, blest reveries aside.

> *Dance under the stars; dance under the stars; tonight!*
> *Live and move in me; love and cherish me; tonight!*

Feeling; now I'm feeling; free and alive while the whole world is turning.
Hoping; now I'm hoping; open and warm as the ashes are burning;
Healing; I am healing; all of my wounds as your love, me is filling;

Lady; lovely lady; make the world new with your love never failing;

> *Open up your heart; open up your heart; tonight!*
> *Feel inside your soul; a candle glows warm; and bright...*

A chilling beauty filled the air as her tender and enchanting voice danced across the still lake. The stars above shimmered in the unfathomable depths of the lake below, and the sacred grounds assumed the feel of an island floating through space. Her full melodious voice, vaulted, unbounded, and emotive, brought great warmth and many a tear to the enraptured audience. Their fondness for Aretta's performance grew because of their own fondness for their goddess, Esharah, who was often portrayed in such a lovely consoling manner (the Lydian equivalent was the planet and goddess Venus who often graced the night sky throughout the year). As Luna listened, her heart yearned for that tender warmth from on high, so much she began to believe in an end to all suffering, emptiness, and pain. After Aretta finished, the Yimisa gave a loud approving shout.

Many more performances followed: stories of love, danger, and war; much music; and wild dancing. The festivity lasted well into the night, but Luna retired earlier than most, being rather exhausted but also anxious for the following day when her mother was expected to arrive.

That night she dreamed once more about the devouring leopard. But the festival and most notably Aretta's haunting ballad nurtured a fresh hope and an inner warmth that, unknown to her, prepared her for a new outcome.

The sky was dark with gloom, and a shadowy cave lay across a grassy plain. The tall grasses rattled as the wind rushed through, parting a way directly to the cave. The rain began to pour down violently, and lightning flashed clear across the sky. With unprecedented determination, Luna courageously moved along that path toward the dark cave: this time she refused to be the prey.

She gathered some vines that lay tangled about in the grasses. Wrapping them tightly around her bare hands and hardening her grip with a gentle pull, the vines bit firmly into her hands and burned slightly at the edges of her palms.

She walked confidently toward her prey with her hands low and stretched about shoulder length apart.

The light flashed, and the creature's grizzly face appeared for an instant. He pounced, but Luna caught him by the throat. His paws soon also became tangled in the mass of vines, which suddenly began multiplying ferociously. Around and around, the vines circled until the beast was totally devoured.

The lightning flashed once more and a burial plot appeared, a tangled mass of vines covering the fallen beast, flowering pink. Moments before waking, Luna walked away. As she walked, she felt an uneasy feeling as her attention was drawn watchfully backward toward the concealed foe.

XXIV

"PARTING IS SUCH SWEET SORROW"

The following afternoon, Anna arrived and straightway, searched out her child.

Luna spotted her as her mother approached the deep pool of water into which she was about to jump. "Mom!" she called out from the tall rock. "You came!" Luna plummeted into the water, diving head first.

"Oh my God," Anna gasped as she slapped Hal across the face, "my baby can swim!"

Anna ran to her soaking wet daughter and stole a hug.

"What a crazy Uncle you have!" she exclaimed. "He came bursting through my front door, panting like a madman, and telling me all sorts of wild jabbering fibs to get me to walk for nearly a week to this dreadful jungle of his, and I followed him. If I were just ten years older, that trip would have killed me. Now look at you … no, you cannot stay here, so let's go home."

"I had to tell her that you wouldn't leave," Hal reported, "she didn't believe anything else, that crazy woman."

"Mom," Luna remarked aggressively, "we're not going back to the city. We have to go stay with Aretta."

"She really is here?" Anna questioned in disbelief.

"Yes," Aretta affirmed as she approached, "we have to get to safety. Asralon is no longer safe for anyone."

"Hal," Anna turned trustingly to her brother, "I don't want to leave." She thought back to the times seventeen years ago when her husband Rowan was still with her. Tears began to fill her eyes as she struggled to let her memories go.

"You can't stay," insisted Luna, "I missed you, and I don't want us to go back there."

"Well, I have made it halfway to 'God knows where'; I guess a little further won't do me any harm."

"I'll lead the way for you tomorrow," Hal concluded. "I'll stay with you until we reach Great Bottom Loop. From there I'll have to head south, but I'll meet back up with you after two months at Stalsbury Castle. Sister, get plenty of rest tonight; you won't be resting as comfortably the next few days."

"A real castle," Anna remarked, "that should be a treat."

With matters settled, they all departed and went about making their final preparations. Hal met with the chief to ask about the scouting soldiers and chat. Luna spent the evening with her new friends. She promised she'd never forget them and would visit as soon as she could. "Perhaps I'll have a horse next time," she added.

After thanking her friends, especially Ilana, for their support, she began to cry. They huddled close and embraced her heartily. "I'm a mess," Luna sobbed.

Ilana raised Luna's chin. "A beautiful one," she declared as she looked in her downcast eyes. "Don't forget I told you," she added. "You'll see."

They embraced one last time before some of the youth broke away and went about their evening duties. At last, Ilana remained and said, "I don't know how I'll ever make it without you. I don't want to say goodbye."

They sat together quietly until the stars slowly began to pop out, and gradually a canopy of thousands of stars hung high in the infinite expanse above them.

XXV

THE GATE OF FIRE

In the morning the small company prepared to leave. Many a long goodbye and thank you were exchanged between the parting friends, and during the drama, Luna recalled a Lydian proverb that was engraved on a monument back home:

> *Seasons change;*
> *The moon will wax and she will wane;*
> *At the end of day, you remain;*
> *Seasons change.*

'What a dreary thought,' pondered Luna. It seemed like a hopeless paradox. As they left the camp, putting their first foot forward by early afternoon, the sounds of the busy tribe dwindled into silence, and suddenly the four travelers found themselves all alone and surrounded by the mighty and lonesome forest. Suddenly, the noninclusive calls of birds, the evasions of squirrels or other creatures, and the unattainably lofty treetops sparked a sensation of isolation and abandonment rather than that of wonder. They were embarking on a new journey that would entirely change the course of their lives.

The meandering path through the forest descended slowly in a southwesterly direction, until they reached the main trail, which winded its way along the trough of the valley toward the Gate of Fire. The initial descent to the main trail was quite gradual, but after reaching the main trail, the elevation dropped quickly. Furthermore, the forest there underwent a drastic change. Being much lower, the valley was filled with beech trees and alders, and as the climate grew warmer and drier at the lower altitudes, they began to see trees like oak, maple, and elm. There, unshielded by any outlying mountain ranges, a constant stiff breeze whisked through the wide vale.

As they descended still more, and the valley narrowed, the trees thinned out and mostly willows, tufts of reed grass and small shrubs dotted the rocky ground of the sandstone passage. It was here that they caught their first good glimpse of the outer flatlands. Out at the mountain's edge, toward the setting sun, stood several towering sandstone pillars with softly rounded tops. Each of the spires had its own curious shape and orientation, and many of them appeared to be tall stacks of large boulders. Those round rocky fringes in the foreground concealed the enormity of the drop in elevation to the plains below. Once they reached the open area near the rocky fringe of the mountains, they made camp for the night.

During the few hours before nightfall, the company walked about the open-air cathedral that they found themselves in. The floor was wide and mostly flat with a few massive boulders creating some undulations, high platforms, and deep crevices. Along the sides of the open space, they were surrounded by a nearly vertical wall of solid rock with visible strata and narrow stress cracks running in various directions. The only passage was back through the forest behind them or onward and beyond the narrow gate to the west, which lay between two tall centrally-located rock outcroppings: the gate of fire.

Beyond the gate, they saw the colossus of the ancient king, Boagerus, looking south. He stood at a right angle to the lay of the main trail, proud and tall, feet spread shoulder-length apart, eyes slightly guarded by his right arm, which stretched directly out from his body into the vertical and horizontal plane of the figure's heart, and left arm cocked beneath the said shoulder. His shielding hand was held vertically with fingers outstretched and palm facing south. Beyond him, the whole world appeared to stretch endlessly, and nearly a quarter mile below waved a golden sea of grassland containing not a soul in sight.

The monument was several stories tall, the hand alone exceeding the height of a tall man. It was erected in memory of their first king who, as legend says, fell in that very place from exhaustion and in vision, saw himself standing there looking southward. A powerful fire dragon had approached him to counsel him, at the sight of which he raised his right arm in the above manner to shield his eyes from the effulgent glory of his counselor.

The mood that night was solemn and quiet, and shortly after the sunset, they were all fast asleep. In the morning, the party made their steep descent, and thoughts of making the trip on horseback quickly vanished from Luna's mind as they stumbled and struggled for purchase on the nearly shear rocks that paved the way. Each steep descent gave way to some pleasantly flat ground, but in some places the elevation dropped sharply for ten to twenty feet. If not for Hal bringing a rope, the journey would have been impossible, especially for Anna who was well into her fifty third year.

"Are you crazy?" she often protested before being lowered to the next platform.

After completing some of the more difficult descents, a smile crept onto her hardened face, but she never let on that she actually enjoyed her incredible feats. At those times she wagged her head and teased, smiling, "Never again, Hal! Never!" or "Wait till we get to the bottom, boy. You just wait."

The descent took just over a quarter of the day, and upon reaching the bottom, they had only to traverse a small stretch of wild grassland before reaching the road. After parting their way through the fields for just under an hour, they reached Great Bottom Loop by mid to late afternoon.

The party headed south along the road until they reached a small overgrown path branching off to their right. Here, Great Bottom Loop drew quite near unto the South Road: the road to which Hal was heading. This small branch connected to its partner road after just a forty minute walk; and once there, Hal would head further south toward Aeoglas, a bridge town on the southern border where he had some business to conduct. Hal promised them his speedy return and started to say goodbye to his beloved companions as he turned to face his lonely conduit.

"This is it," he lamented. "I'm going to miss you all so much. Maybe I will settle down after all. Who knows?"

He turned back to give Luna a big hug.

"Once again, you have amazed me," he said as he wrapped his arms around her. "What can I say?"

"Thanks for taking me, Uncle," Luna replied. "I'm so lucky to have you … I'm going to be okay."

"I know," he said as tears welled up in his eyes. He pinched his lips together for a moment and stepping back, he looked into her eyes. "I think I'm the lucky one."

They moved close again for another embrace until Hal moved on to his sister.

"That's my little sister," he said. "I knew you could do it."

"Oh, just hurry on and get back to us," she replied as she playfully tromped his foot.

After a short warm embrace, he moved on to the queen. Bowing before her, he said, "I bid you well, fair queen."

She moved close and stooping to grab his hands, she said as Hal rose to his feet, "Thank you for guiding us, Hal. Have a safe journey."

With that, they parted ways and the three women continued on the road for about a mile, heading southeasterly. Anna was the oldest in the company, followed by Aretta who was just forty-two; and the long flat road and the warmth of the sun was a welcome change from the rocky heights and the cool damp forest above, especially for the now exhausted Anna.

"We could reach Stalsbury by late evening," Aretta said hopefully, "but perhaps we should rest a bit, and continue on in the morning." She pointed to a grove of mighty oak trees just a short distance ahead on their right.

"Sure," Luna agreed, "we could all use a little rest after that climb."

"Alright, we'll spend the night here and travel again in the morning."

"Good."

"Just show me where to sit," chimed Anna.

XXVI

GARDENS, GARDENS EVERYWHERE!

They rested for the night and in the morning woke to a passing shower. The heavy, sudden onslaught drenched them; and the women all ducked for cover with laughter filling their faces as they looked at each other hiding under shirts and baggage, already sopping wet. It passed within minutes though, and soon enough the warm morning sun beamed forth and kissed the countryside. After a short meal, the ladies packed up and headed for their destination.

The road continued onward straight and flat, and all the while, the massive peak of Mount Youlden towered high above them and far to their left. After about an hour of walking, the steep inimical cliffs on their left terminated abruptly, and the road turned eastward to pass them by. Rounding the corner of the last high rock, the company caught a view of the kindlier eastern country. A soft, wide, green gully lay first to their left, cradled by the steep surrounding rock, followed by another steep spur, then another soft gully still, while each successive spur grew softer and more sprawling, and each gully, shallower, until, far off in the distance, the mountainside became quite soft and even. On their right and across the road to their left, the grassland continued to where it licked the foothills of the mount. The company followed the road, now heading nearly east; and before long, the jagged summit passed over their shoulders. Here, the gentle slope of the mountainside turned completely green, and simultaneously – the time of day being late afternoon – Stalsbury came into view. Off in the distance the Stalsbury vineyards could be seen with their vines neatly stretched out in numerous long rows.

"A vineyard!" Luna said excitedly. "I should have known." Stalsbury had quite a reputation for their fine wines.

The old stone estate, which sat close to the mountain slope, followed the lay of the east road and encompassed it. A ten foot high stone wall bordered it on every side; and incrementally, roughly every quarter mile, an unoccupied guard tower stood built into the wall. In times of war or danger, the great east and west arches would be closed in defense, thereby blocking the road; but for the most part, road traffic had flowed freely and uninterrupted through Stalsbury for the past twenty years.

Shortly, the group reached the western arch, and after passing it by, they unofficially reached their new home. The open spaces around them were tastefully adorned with an idyllic arrangement of fruit trees, small flower and vegetable gardens, quaint stone sheds and homes, and a sprawling blanket of soft green grass, among which were a few servants, busily pulling loads or cheerfully soaking up the soft breeze that bounded nimbly about the grounds. Moving on, the buildings drew closer and eventually began to take on larger and more magnificent proportions while still maintaining the same elegant and charming air of carefree bliss. Every space was ingeniously beautified, affecting a sense that a labyrinth of gardens wove its way around every corner and created a world of beauty and wonder that stood just waiting to be explored.

Halfway into Stalsbury and still to the left, the main residence rose magnificently above its surroundings; and all roads seemed to flow in its direction. It was surrounded foursquare, by a thick wall, above which, walkways enclosed by round white-marble balustered railings and adjacent bridges to the main residence laid.

Below this network of bridges were streets and cellars and gardens with stone sculptures, fountains and topiary. Archways proliferated throughout the entire nexus, allowing diverse sized roads to pass beneath; and there, near the arches, various ornate plaques, reliefs, antefixes, statues, miniatures, and columns were set, whose carvings of beasts, plants, cherubs, and the like elegantly adorned the entire system.

The main road, however, continued along to the south of this complex of gardens and bridges, and as Aretta and her friends moved along the south-most wall, they saw no arches or entrances, simply one solid mass of wall crowned with a marble rail, having one deviation: a large gate, protruding. Just inside the wide, open gate, a broad, three-tiered marble staircase ascended and met the long central approach to the Great Entrance Hall.

At that gate, Aretta and her company were greeted by a welcoming party whose job included inquiring into the nature of their visit.

Aretta had wisely disguised herself and instructed Anna to speak in their behalf. Anna didn't pay much attention to the instructions, and approaching the welcoming party said, "The queen wishes to see Lady Ellen."

The greeter looked close at Anna and smiled. "Oh, sure!" he bantered. "Top of the stairs. Straight ahead. Can't miss her."

As they climbed, Aretta whispered, "Anna, dear, I'm trying to hide; please don't tell anyone that the queen is here – Oh, thank God he thought you meant yourself."

"That's what I meant," Anna replied. "I always wanted to pretend to be queen."

"Mom!" Luna scolded.

Upon reaching the top of the stairs, they looked north across the central complex, and at its northern extremity stood the tall manor of Lady Ellen, and beyond, the soft hillside with endless rows of vines. The view from the top of the stairs offered a good look at the marvelous order and symmetry of the entire quadrate system.

Anna and Luna were both spellbound. During the past twenty minutes, they had been walking along, admiring what was in fact – collectively speaking – the most exquisite work of art that they had ever seen; and this was soon to be their new home! Near the entrance, Aretta spotted the widowed lady of the house, Ellen, dressed in a lovely, full yellow and red dress, overlooking a group of masons who were erecting a monument of her late husband, Victor, in the gardens. The artist had spent three years on the sculpture, and it was finally ready. Proceeding no further, the ladies lingered at the nearest flat stone rail, from which, in the interest of looking busy, they pretended to admire the view of the gardens; but to their chagrin, they found themselves poised directly over a quirky looking rock garden of the sort that only Victor could love.

"What a lovely looking … uh …?" Anna stammered as she stared at a large spherical stone with a hole cut through its center. "Luna?"

"Why yes … it's lovely," she added as Aretta interrupted.

"It looks like Lady Ellen is finished with her business. You stay here, and I'll approach her."

"If you don't mind, I think I'll be walking yonder," Anna said as she pointed toward a bench overlooking a lovely rose garden.

"Fine, I'll be right back," Aretta said kindly as she walked off.

Lady Ellen was about the age of the queen, and as children, she and Ellen had grown up together just north of Asralon, in a lovely little village near the border. After marrying, they went their separate ways, but she and Aretta never lost touch with each other. They often exchanged letters and never failed to stop in on one another if they were near or passing through. She was a tall and beautiful, altruistic woman, but had little tolerance for mistakes; and though lovely, her aspect often seemed cold, and her disposition, aloof. Capable of being quite charming and holding engaging discourse as she was, her social charm quickly deteriorated and turned to scolding when she perceived something about her gone amiss. Nonetheless, her generosity always prevailed in the end, and few had any reason to fear that her displeasure would endure.

Oh, how strange to approach the best of friends in such a covert manner: creeping after her like a stalker. Near the stone pavement before the mansion, Aretta closed in on her "fleeing" friend, and reaching out, tapped Ellen from behind upon her shoulder. Startled, Ellen turned back to see and with a scowl, slowly ran her palm across her "infected" shoulder while she turned back to get on her way. Making the next few steps, she suddenly stopped after realizing who it was that touched her. She turned about with a look of bewilderment and asked, "Aretta?"

Aretta, blushing, answered her sheepishly, "Yes."

"What happened?"

The two stood and talked together for about an hour, as Aretta tried to explain what was happening. Explicitly, she related the details following Thaddeus' death: Nathan's public execution of Balto, his attempt to usurp the throne by force, his voluntary expulsion and subsequent return, her flight, and so on. Ellen's eyes grew wide.

"You haven't heard about General Indow then?"

"No, what happened?"

"I'll tell you later, but the gist of it is that he accused the nearby tribe of acts of violence, which, after investigation, proved false, the end of the matter being exile to the east, never to return, under the pain of death."

"Well that awful general, what was he thinking?"

"Indeed. Yet, clearly, we have ourselves a rather spunky king, wouldn't you say?"

"That isn't the half of it."

"Aretta, you are still the queen and the boy's mother, surely you can handle this."

"I'm afraid I'm at a loss, which is why I came here."

"No!"

"What would you have me do?"

"There must be something."

"And risk a civil war? I'm certain that Nathan will not tolerate my opposition. And how could I justify such a conflict to my exponents; when the first blood is spilled and my men are lying dead, will they not lose heart?"

"They'll have you.... Oh, what am I saying? I'm not suggesting a civil war. It simply looks like a domestic dispute at this point. What would stop anyone from wondering why you couldn't work out an agreement? So why can't you?"

"I just can't."

"You? Can't?"

"Not now – I don't know what to do right now."

"Fair enough, but what's to come of it when everyone thinks you're dead or missing? Will you act then?"

"I don't know."

"What is wrong, Aretta? This isn't like you. You don't think you have enough loyalists in the kingdom who would uphold you?"

"Of course I do, but that's what I mean by civil war. It will come to arms; I know it."

"Then let it. After you oust his – what – three hundred proponents in one whole day, he gets a speedy lesson, and you resume your reign."

But Aretta was convinced that destiny would have its way with her no matter what she contrived or failed to contrive. "No," she insisted. "I've done all I can do at this point, the only thing that makes any sense to me is waiting."

"More like hiding."

"I wanted to stay here with you Ellen, but it seems that my stay would be too difficult for you. Please, at least accept my two friends. I am bound to them."

Aretta pointed toward Luna and Anna, who were looking about the grounds from the bridges.

"This is so exciting, Mother!" Luna said as she embraced herself.

"I'm sorry – I'm ready to go home. It is a lovely place, but too much for me."

"Oh, Mom, you are so simple," Luna teased. She looked over toward Aretta who was standing near Lady Ellen. "What do you think they're talking about?"

"Probably all sorts of silly stuff … Look at her, looking over here right now, wondering what sort of riffraff the queen dragged along with her."

"Oh, she's calling us over, I'm so excited."

As Luna and Anna made their way over toward them, Ellen continued speaking with Aretta. "My friend; my dear, dear friend; do forgive me. I want you to stay here, I do. I mean that sincerely. We'll have great times together, I promise."

"No, you're right, I'm expecting too much," Aretta responded, nearly in tears.

The other two arrived.

Turning toward them, Aretta assured, "Ellen is eager to make your acquaintance, she'll be delighted to have you here … besides she's been looking for some vinedressers."

"But I've never dressed vines before," confessed Luna.

"Oh, that's quite alright, my fine young lady. You must be Luna, right?" Ellen said as she cordially offered her hand. Luna accepted it timidly, almost afraid to look up into Ellen's eyes.

"And you must be Anna?" she asked turning toward Luna's mother. "In just a few moments, I'll have someone show you to your quarters. You'll be staying in the main residence with me."

"Do you think you'll be comfortable?" asked Aretta, turning toward Luna.

"Perfectly," replied Luna.

"Good. I'm going to be departing shortly. I hope to see you when I visit again."

"Going?" Luna questioned in shock. Her countenance was visibly shaken.

Aretta was moved by the sight. She looked toward Ellen who stared at her bearing a somewhat cockeyed expression. She smiled back at Ellen, at last softened by her friend's sincerity.

"You really want me to stay?" she asked, turning toward the downcast Luna in disbelief.

"Oh yes," Luna retorted, perking up. "It wouldn't be the same without you."

"Thank you," Aretta replied. "You don't know how much that warms my heart. I'll stay; besides, I have a feeling that you're not the only one who'd miss me."

"I didn't say anything about missing anyone," Anna asserted.

Ellen and Aretta embraced each other affectionately. "Thank you Ellen," she conceded. "If you don't mind?"

"Are you kidding? I couldn't ask for a more pleasant surprise. Now, let's go on and find you some places, shall we?"

The four women walked inside together through the front entrance; and walking across the Valencia-yellow marble hall and red gold-fringed runners, they turned left beyond the marble stair-case; and passing below it, entered a red carpeted hall richly decorated with elaborate stone wainscoting, chair rails, friezes and an ornate wood-crafted lacunar ceiling. Halfway down the hall after turning right, they entered a smaller enclosed scissor staircase; and going to the second floor, they turned right and walked down along the red carpet toward the end of the hall to the two rooms where Anna and Luna would stay. After pointing out to Luna and Anna the location of their rooms, the company turned left and followed the hall down toward the front of the building; turning left again, they continued along toward the center of the residence where they found Aretta's room.

"I warmly welcome all of you to Stalsbury! Now, I apologize, but I really must be going," Lady Ellen explained. "Aretta knows where everything is, she can show you around. See you at dinner?"

"Sure," they all replied. "Thank you."

Ultimately, Stalsbury proved to be a safe haven for the three girls, and for Luna and Anna, it was a welcome change from their tiny residence in the poor parts of Asralon. There was so much to do, and the work was refreshing. And even though Luna remained a little apprehensive about going about alone, she still felt quite secure. The other residents were friendly, yet knew how to keep a comfortable distance; and Luna and Anna found that they could comfortably continue their lives with little disturbance. The years that followed would prove that their move couldn't have come at a more opportune time.

XXVII

TEN YEARS BEHIND YOU

After two months passed with not a word of his mother's whereabouts, Nathan assumed her dead. So, he held a memorial for her at the royal palace, where the incessant wailing of the mourners drove nearly any grief he may have felt clear from his heart.

Aretta, abdicating completely, surrendered to her new lot; and upon hearing news of her purported death, made little effort to make the truth public. So certain she had become of the truthfulness of her vision after hearing about Luna's rape at the hands of her son, that she saw little reason to risk a correspondence. Many times she began a letter or envisioned herself speaking together with him; but she'd quickly rip the missive to shreds, and the visions ended in disaster. She often searched herself for answers to her enigmatic predicament, and after her introspection left her in dolorous melancholy, she woolgathered up the false hope of a wise confidant to whom she could disclose her secret. So much did she yearn to rid herself of the guilt-infested sense of responsibility caused by her remiss, debauched clemency. Owning the truth publicly was out of the question, for if on the one hand, nobody believed her incredible testimony, then they would think her mad; but on the other hand, credulity would inevitably lead to incrimination and an abhorrent public disdain that would burgeon with each passing day and every tragic report: a burden she could scarce carry in addition to her already torturous guilt. And worse still, was the possibility that the contest would come to arms and Lydian blood would be shed. She wanted more than anything to save her kingdom, but it seemed that no amount of love or goodness could reverse what she had willfully set in motion. Those frequent desperate searches often ended with her despairing for her life, and wishing that she could give it up in exchange for the security of her beloved Lydia.

Soon after news of the queen's "death" had reached Stalsbury, Hal returned from Aeoglas with news of a battle that broke out for control of the bridge there. A few days after his arrival in the southern town, a feeble assault was made on the garrison of Lydians that protected the bridge on the south side. The southern bordering nation, Caria, was being levied with a heavy toll that was instituted by an enterprising commander who had occupied that post. He imagined that he would take advantage of the general lack of order that was experienced following Thaddeus' death. His delusions of grandeur were short lived however, when the neighboring tribes demanded the man's head and stoutly refused to pay the toll. The Lydian soldiers refused to betray their own officer, whereupon the angry foreigners stormed the bridge. They were quickly cut down by the defending squad; but the battle soon became an eyesore for the new king, and peace would never be restored, as a result of Nathan's proud refusal to pay restitution to his militarily "inferior" neighbors. The Carians refused to be placated by empty apologies or even the removal of Commander Olan from his post, who incidentally became a willing puppet to the king's waving carrot.

Nathan had found that anyone who he could manipulate with promises of wealth or power, made for the most obedient of servants, and he jokingly referred to them as his dogs.

Oh yes, Nathan's rule degenerated from bad to worse, and he squandered the nation's resources in just ten years. And in every direction, Nathan, prey to his own pride and rapacity, created enemies and instigated alienation, while the Lydians, who by and

large were victims of a nationalistic blindness, grumbled offens-
ively at their disgruntled neighbors.

Over the years, news of the nation's downfall began to trickle
into Stalsbury from every corner of Lydia, but few were intuitive
enough to see where the state of affairs was headed: enthralled as
they were by their then hedonistic lifestyle – enlarging their
estates, undertaking extravagant projects, acquiring new habits,
depleting the nation's resources, and consequently borrowing large
sums of money to fuel their machinations.

As the reports poured in, Aretta maintained with great difficultly,
a façade of her former grace and poise; but within a few years, her
former days of ease and delight slid unfathomably into abysmal
darkness, becoming artificial memories of a preceding impalpable
lifetime. Further vexing her was the indelible anamnesis of her
desperate flight from Asralon following her son's rise to power,
which led invariably to that bizarre yet dazzling moment in the
mountain where all her senses unequivocally faded into black and
something otherworldly took over. It perplexed her how alive and
full of orgasmic delight she was in at that moment. The event
alone cast a long shadow that seemed to blacken the happiness
that she thought she had masterfully attained her whole life prior.
Even the love she shared with Thaddeus paled in comparison to
the inexplicable bliss she had felt during that night. All else seemed
dead and lifeless; only her early childhood memories held a close
second to that epiphany.

It took those several years of agonizing and bemusement before
she willingly admitted failure. Little did she know, but she clung
so tenaciously to her own enticing dreams of love and harmony
that the simple, naïve answers would never find her, until the near
the end. However, Aretta's façade was convincing enough – so
much it was truly innate, although under such duress, it *felt* forced
– that even Luna acquired an extraordinary gracefulness, which

she wore like an uncomfortable garment but had nevertheless assimilated from her frequent association with the more refined Aretta. And though Luna bore a secret of her own, she would hardly remember it until the fateful tenth year of Nathan the king.

XXVIII

THE BREAKING POINT

During that tenth year, fear could visibly be seen on the visiting messengers and guests of Stalsbury. Rumours of an economic collapse were circulating, and when the first of the penniless noblemen began to pour into the mansion – faces white and hearts in a fit of passion – the reports were suddenly believable. Several of them were held accountable for the mismanagement of the nation's wealth and recounted how they were forcibly driven from their estates by military henchmen.

Prior to their expulsion, Nathan – still having his spell cast over Lydia – in a public address concerning their dire straights, denounced and named the principle "defalcators" responsible for their then deplorable state. Many a reputable financier and statesmen's name was accompanied by boos and hisses from the trepid throng as Nathan enumerated them along with their various denunciations and "remunerations." Actually unwilling to make the necessary cuts in spending, Nathan surreptitiously attempted to make up for the nation's shortage by vampirishly seizing the wealth and property of the detracted statesmen.

The nation had been enjoying unprecedented prosperity for much of the years prior, and wealth and luxury were pouring into the streets. There were invisible repercussions however, blowing holes beneath the surface of the apparently stable extravagance. Competition grew fierce and drove the prices of the basic necessities of life down. Consequently, only those who could keep the cost of production low could remain afloat. Farming practices became more irresponsible, and hired workers became seasonal and were paid less and less. Only the greediest of suppliers – be it grain, minerals, wood, textiles, or anything else – could maintain their luxurious lifestyle without taking on loans. True to form, foolish aspiring entrepreneurs entered on the scene to outdo their opponents with cheaper labor and cheaper goods, thereby setting the precedent for the rest of the struggling purveyors: the ultimate result being a marked increase in disproportionate wealth. However, many unheralded advances in technology were presented during these years, such as the Elethian Plow for instance, which was created using new forging techniques: its design resulting in increased agricultural production.

Yet, soon enough, the poor became extremely poor; the "rich", slaves to the truly rich; and the land, a hopeless victim of senseless greed, until near the tenth year, the cities seethed with crime and violence. Yet the tractable impoverished consoled themselves with empty dreams of making it big and getting their piece of the pie, while the feasting remnant's taste for luxury blinded them to the obvious neglect that was seething across the cities. And of course, everyone had to pay the piper.

And he, worst of all, consumed the nation's wealth and youth at an alarming rate, with his endless military operations to crush some uprising, build some bridge, or secure a border. Further, Nathan's personal guard numbered into the hundreds, all of them seasoned soldiers who were rewarded generously for their obedient service. The military increased their mining operations and in the wake, the forests were callously uprooted and wasted.

So it was in that tenth year, during Lady Ellen's yearly autumn harvest celebration that Luna heard the most disturbing report yet. Toward evening, she was standing near a planter in the center of the Great Entrance Hall, when it all began.

The hall itself was exquisite: a light yellow floor, with a large central medallion of the sun and a host of other patterns inlaid; a wide white stone staircase on the western side; marble planters containing exotic broad-leafed plants; and best of all, a large northern wall of windows offering a gorgeous vista of the vineyards and mountains. Having her back toward the large windows and looking toward the entrance, she saw a man burst through the front doors in a state of panic. It was a servant of the chief treasurer; and close on his heels, it seemed that all the shadows of Lydia entered with him. Lady Ellen caught sight of him from where she stood near the stairs. Rushing over, she passed below the front balcony past one of the six burnt orange supporting pillars to meet him; and upon reaching him, she put her arm around him. Thereafter, she gently guided him into a private vestibule in the southwest corner and closed the door behind her. Luna slowly and curiously drew close, even hoping to help; so much was she moved by the discomfited look of the newcomer. After reaching the door, she heard the voices faintly coming through it. Drawing closer, she heard what they were saying:

Ellen: "Executed?"

Servant: "Yes, he refused to leave and denied that he handled the nation's money wastefully. The soldiers cut him down on the spot. I fled immediately."

Ellen: "Are you in any danger?"

Servant: "No, but my lord's place is now occupied...."

Luna drew away. It sounded awful. She had heard the various reports of the nation's decline abundantly these past few months, but this was the first she heard of an execution. The shades that crept in moments ago felt closer and somewhat heckling: she stepped outside for a smoke.

After about half an hour, Lady Ellen emerged.

Taking a place in the center of the hall she spoke to the hundred or so who were gathered. Her voice, now hollow, quivered with urgency:

"My friends, I don't know how to begin, but in this time, more than ever, we need to stick together. I …" she stopped herself short of speaking anything that could be considered seditious, "… I hope … we can all take a serious look at where Lydia is headed. I think we all know that if we all join together, we can still turn things around. I have just heard news of terrible things. Good men are losing their lives. Our whole nation is in jeopardy. Stalsbury may be a safe haven now; but even here, the widespread poison will eventually attain."

Luna caught the tail end of the speech and found that Ellen's words did little to exorcise the demons that now lurked throughout their once impregnable abode.

In a tizzy, Ellen deserted her dumbfounded guests, forcing them to muddle their own way through her short and inconclusive plaint, and searched out Aretta whom she now harbored with exacerbating resentment. She had had enough of Aretta's hiding.

Aretta was taking a walk in the western garden with some of the few trusted friends that she had acquired over the years, when Lady Ellen found her, pulled her aside, and ducked her under one of the taller, old apple trees nearby.

"You need to do something about this!" she demanded. "If you come out of hiding, the whole nation could rally to your side." The plan felt a little better than it sounded. Really, the thought of a long forgotten queen rising up and leading a band of peasants to victory against the formidable army of the state, seemed a bit outlandish.

"Damn it, Aretta, enough is enough," she ceded. Aretta watched as Ellen began to break down.

"I'm sorry Ellen," she replied, thoroughly ashamed, "I missed my chance twenty-seven years ago."

"That's not your fault," replied Ellen, thinking that Aretta was blaming herself for Nathan's behaviour. "You couldn't have known."

"But I did," Aretta confessed. "The night he was conceived, I knew what he'd do. I could have stopped him before he was born, but I didn't: I chose him."

"What are you talking about?"

Aretta recounted to Ellen the dream, the still river, the berry, everything.

Ellen's tone changed, and a look of disgust filled her face. "You did what?" she scolded. "How could you be so stupid?"

"Ahgh!" she growled as she stormed off.

Standing alone in the dark, in the open air, with the wind and the trees watching her with a soothing indifference, Aretta nearly ran once more. And she would have, had it not been for a sudden thud followed by a loud shriek on the near side of Ellen's mansion. Aretta ascended the nearby stairs to see what was wrong and discovered the mangled body of the frightened servant who showed up that evening. A few ladies were gathered around chatting, before the terror stricken man plummeted from the fourth story to his death.

Aretta searched out Ellen, making no attempt to conceal herself. Finding her, she said, "Ellen, there's been a suicide!"

Making her way outside, Ellen watched as several persons gathered about, and the chief groundskeeper stood in amazement.

"Lady Ellen? You don't want to see this," he cautioned.

Ellen turned about in tears with her hands clasped about her nose and mouth. Squeamish, she ran off, and Aretta stayed behind to settle and divert the turbulent crowd. Happily, no one recognized her as being the queen, because later that night, Aretta sat together with Ellen to sort things out; and Ellen, who was quite shaken by the catastrophic events of the day, had a change of heart. She hadn't the stomach for death and violence.

"I can't let anyone know you're here," she realized. "I'm not prepared for a war ... Aretta ... you need to stay in hiding. For those few short moments that you were exposed, I thought I'd lost the whole of Stalsbury. I'm sorry for berating you, Aretta."

"You're right Ellen. I need to do something ... before it's too late."

"I know, but now I'm scared."

They held each other close for several minutes, before Ellen dismissed her friend.

"Please, hold your cover," she insisted.

Aretta had no intentions of blowing her cover. She had simply run to help; it was instinctive: natural. Still in so, she once again began to think over what she *could* do if she came out of hiding. So after thinking the matter through laboriously, she started a series of pseudonymous writings in hopes of reversing the injurious trends that had become so widespread: an act she had been thinking about for a long time. They ultimately proved to be too little, too late.

Luna, however, walked about that night as if haunted by some distant ghost, until she settled in for the night. In the still moments before she drifted off to sleep, a forgotten memory crept from the recesses of her mind. She sat up instantly.

"No!" she whispered as the realization struck her. She had already been told that Lydia would be ruined; and she had killed the child who could have saved the nation. She sat for a moment and tried to absorb the gravity of what she had done. By now her child would have been nine years old, and what would he have been like? Would he have been some kind of savior: a genius, a wizard?

"Could he really have been that important?" she pondered. But the fact of the matter was that her son was not, and wondering about what could have been had no merit to her whatsoever. However, a burdensome sense of responsibility was kindled in that hour, and in addition, a fateful seed of thought that would take several years to come to fruition began to germinate.

That year brought great changes to the lives of the Lydians; and in the coming years, Ellen had to cut back more and more, yet she refused to let a single servant go. Living in her self-sustained fort-ress made that easier than one might imagine; Stalsbury was the sort of place that could weather even a complete collapse of the central government. However, sacrifices were still required on the part of everyone, and Ellen's sense of solidarity stood the test.

XXIX

A DAY OF RECKONING

With each passing year and every bad report, the secrets of the two women wore at them. After news of some failed uprising or some execution reached them, it was common not to see either of them for a few days except wandering about in some lonely place: subdued. Sometimes weeks would go by before that haunting and irresistible light could be seen in Luna's eyes.

It was common in such times to see the Lydians dejected or somber, but Aretta was never known to balk under any weight. Her veneer had cracked and was near to disintegrating.

The nation as a whole fared no better. By Nathan's twelfth year, the larger uprisings began to subside into small hopeless skirmishes: the stiff reprisals for insubordination infused that much fear into all of Lydia. By his fifteenth year, the dispirited populace was nearly catatonic.

That year, in mid-April, after a restless sleep, Luna awoke following repeated dreams about her unborn child. The dreams felt rather unnatural and orchestrated; a forced smile was plastered across Luna's face while she laid on her back, turning left and then right, holding the young blond infant just above her head as he gazed about the room inquisitively. The same scene haunted her repeatedly, till toward early morning when she sat up in her bed. It wasn't till then, that the gravity really hit her.

'I took a life,' she pondered as she looked up at her hands and pictured the warm soft hands of her imagined son.

'He would have been warm and alive and … he would have smiled as the sun hit his face,' she thought. Suddenly tears welled up in her eyes, and although presently thirty-two, once again she felt like she was only seventeen.

She ran to Aretta's room to unburden herself. Upon entering, the startled would-be queen sat up slowly from her bed. Luna slowly entered the softly illumined room and passed along the narrow space between the unveiled southern windows and Aretta's bed. The third quarter moon, who was then at her height hung there like a phantom. The moonlight passed through the sheer folds of Luna's elegant blue flowing nightgown as she tiptoed past the window. Aretta's face and resting place were alighted indistinctly by the soft blue light that filled the room. Luna seated herself midway along the edge of the soft bed and faced the large south window. She took a deep breath, during which Aretta detected that Luna was a little choked up with tears.

"What's wrong?" Aretta tenderly asked with her voice a little groggy.

"It's terrible," Luna sniffled.

"All along, people were dying and people needed someone … He was just a baby, a little baby …" her tears began to flow more abundantly. "And I … he could have stopped all this … I killed him."

Aretta was a little confused, "You killed someone?"

"Mmmmgh!" Luna growled. She was angry that she had to explain. "I was going to have a baby. I killed him. I ate Emilia's berry and I killed him!" she shouted.

"I'm sorry," Aretta replied trying to console her. Even so, somewhere inside, she heard herself judging, condemning; but secretly, she held her disgust.

"You don't understand!" Luna continued. "A spirit, a Madonna – I don't know – told me that he would save us; even one of the Yimisa told me something. I ignored it; I didn't want that thing."

Apologizing, Aretta encouraged her to try to get some sleep, telling her it could help; but really, she was wondering how she'd tell Luna her "little" secret. As Luna stood up to leave, Aretta braced herself.

"It's my fault," she admitted. "An angel told me to kill my child before he was born, and I couldn't do it." Luna's blood began to boil. "The angel showed me the evil that he would cause, the destruction, the ruin, if I would have known …"

"You what!" Luna demanded. "You would have kissed him to death, you freak. What's wrong with you?"

"Life is too precious," Aretta explained. "I didn't know …"

"You think life isn't precious to me?" Luna interrupted.

"No!" Aretta shouted. "I didn't know what would happen to ME! I was afraid where such a course would lead ME!" Aretta burst into tears as she finally understood her paradox. "I'm sorry …"

"Don't talk to me again," Luna demanded as she ran from the room and slammed the door behind her.

Standing still in the hall for a moment, she put her hands to her mouth. Nearly forgotten, her painful harbored memories were loosed from their distant shores; and she tried to contain her grief as she ran down the red carpeted halls to her own room, the whole while crying as if it was only yesterday when she had picked herself up from that dark alley.

XXX

THE LAST STAND

Several days prior to this, a messenger came to the castle. He bore a report of a forced evacuation being placed upon all the inhabitants of Asralon. Nathan had finally cracked; seeing his needy disgruntled subjects clawing and begging for help at his doorstep was too much to bear. Besides, he could transform the whole city into a mining operation; it was well known that Asralon sat on a rock bed that was rich with silver ore. He told the Lydians that without the revenue from the silver mine, Lydia would be in danger of invasion from their northern enemy who was now demanding restitution for a fire that had spread across the northern forest of Lydia and razed one of their neighbors' bordering towns. The fire was one of the worst in recent memory; and although it started within the borders of Lydia through no apparent fault of the king or his people, the mistrust and animus that had mounted between his northern neighbor and Lydia through the years roused suspicion to the contrary.

The city was to be leveled on May twelfth, in the fifteenth year of Nathan the king, roughly four weeks from the day that the messenger arrived with the news. The report brought mixed feelings for the residents of Stalsbury. Many wondered where Nathan would stop. Aretta, suddenly feeling that her son's reign had reached the foretold culmination was leveled. Angry, fearful, grieved, and remorseful, she travailed with the news. Within a short time, Aretta became disposed to lead a resistance, but after her falling out with Luna, she became decided. She could no longer live with herself as she watched her nation crumbling before her eyes; against all odds, failure, while valiantly trying to make right her wrongs, was preferable to the rotting guilt that festered within her soul. After discussing the matter with Ellen, she announced her plans to come out of hiding, and lead a resistance into the very heart of the kingdom.

She sent word all throughout the kingdom denouncing Nathan for all his crimes, wastefulness, and negligence. She apologized to her countrymen for her failure to look after their interests and promised personally, to make a stand in the city of Asralon with whomever wished to stand at her side, between the king's armies and their capital city. She sent word to Asralon that all who were courageous and ready should stoutly refuse to leave, and by the preordained day of the twelfth, they would mass together as one outside the gates of the town and form a blockade.

Though she openly exposed herself to the king's wrath, the king reacted with tolerance. He ordered his soldiers to not interfere with the queen's rebellion, promising the frightened captains and generals that her revolt would be short lived. The game had changed, and an old enmity began to surface in the king's breast. Nathan had disgraced nearly everything that his mother held so dear, and he felt a smug pleasure in the work he had done. Now that his mother was still alive, he wished for her game piece to advance: the game had suddenly taken a long desired turn and neared its completion.

During the short weeks ahead, dozens of brave men and women came from towns and villages within the reach of Stalsbury. They brought weapons and clubs: some partisans even being seasoned soldiers. Aretta cringed upon seeing the weapons of war, at the sight of which she suddenly realized that she was leading a military operation. She emphasized to her supporters that violence needed to be considered as a last resort. There was so little time, and so little support, that she didn't expect to pose any sort of military threat; and little more was expected in Asralon. Yet, even a few of the resident soldiers of Stalsbury joined their company and preparations were made hastily. Hal soon arrived and offered his hand, and on the sixth of May, they held a banquet, on the eve of their journey into Asralon.

The company would take Great Bottom Loop for nearly a day's journey east until they reached River Road, which followed the banks of the Sheaglow, the waters of which had cut a gentle "V" shaped valley through the surrounding mountains. The Sheaglow meandered down from the heights of Asralon, falling steadily as it winded its way through the soft hills that came down from Mount Theodore, to the west, and Mount Timothy followed by Edward, on the eastern side. From there, it was a short two days journey into the heart of Asralon. Those roads easily accommodated riders on horseback, and the fifty some odd members of the resistance would ride.

On the eve of their departure Aretta spoke in the great banquet hall:

"I thank you all for your loving support. You have all come, at no little risk to yourselves or your families and friends; and I admire your courage and willingness to make this stand. True, the future of Lydia is obscure, and that affects us all, but no one in this room needs to bear this burden more than me. When Nathan was conceived, I had a choice. A certain dread and foreboding came over me and begged me to end his life, but I refused. It took me far too long to see that I was wrong. I am sorry that I put us all in such a plight." Upon confessing, the expressions on the faces of the gathered appeared dejected and annoyed.

Aretta continued, "My last wish is that whoever makes this journey does it willfully, with no doubt in his or her mind. Please understand that some of us will not return. If you have any reservations, I excuse you from my side; but rest assured, even if I am the only one standing between the king and his plans, I will stand firm."

The gathering one and all stood up and applauded. Aretta had such an irresistible charm and dynamic character that it was hard not to be won over by her manner. Later that evening, Luna, who was also present at the banquet, feeling equally responsible, resolved to join the company in their defense.

Morning came, and the last preparations were made. Horses were saddled; beasts of burden were loaded with food and clothing, and breakfast was served. They one and all set out not long after dawn and made their way eastward toward the Sheaglow passage.

The whole way, Aretta and Luna kept their distance from one another. On setting out, Aretta's now greying hair was arranged neatly and held up in long curls. She wore a lovely flowery dress and a pretty hat. During the journey, she kept a cheerful demeanor and found herself to be surprisingly comfortable in her role, though the task at hand was quite doleful and frightening. She had forgotten how good it felt to have the love, respect, and attention that she was once accustomed to. Her long lost memories of her former regal state returned to her and warmed her heart: she felt young and alive again, loved and appreciated. A sudden inexplicable peace had settled upon her since she came out of hiding, and she felt strangely prepared for even the worst of outcomes.

Luna, on the other hand, was ablaze. Her encounter with Aretta nearly two weeks earlier was not eating at her or impassioning her at all; no, *that* was hardly in her mind. All of the demons that clawed from within, she was poised to reckon with. This was her chance! The hidden fears, the dark memories, the need for redemption after taking her child – she wasn't going to war against some tyrant; she was casting out the devil himself from the heavens of her celestial being. No more – no more! – would she live in fear or regret: this purification was long overdue. Her rich dark hair lay wildly over her shoulders and was crowned with a tattered straw hat that she often wore while working in the vineyards. She wore a brown pair of coveralls, and a beige button up shirt. Overall, her aspect appeared to be formidable and imperious. A fire burned beneath her eyes, and an air of confidence circled about her. She kept to herself during the journey, joyfully cycling her electric vitality with each breath. She would conquer the world!

As they moved eastward, the road ascended slowly upon the foothills of Mount Theodore, whose summit to their left was deceptively high and whose roots sprawled out further south than the other mountains. The party moved along till early afternoon when they reached the crest of a high ridge and the edge of a hardwood forest. Looking back, they could still see the fringes of Stalsbury far below. The incline that they traversed was covered in thick green meadows, and to their left, the snow covered peak of Mount Theodore pierced through a lone cirrus cloud. Below the snowy peak, the sheer grey rock-face plummeted hundreds of feet before reaching a forest of evergreens, reminiscent of the woodland habitat of the Yimisa. The forest continued descending toward their road and became a hardwood deciduous forest by the time it reached them, while the meadow behind them and to their right, continued on its way carpeting the mountainside till it reached a small wooded forest that ran eastward down below. There, a narrow band of linden, maple, hornbeam, and such followed the foot of the mountain and gradually grew thicker and thicker as it drew closer to the higher ground and the river far ahead. Here, the Lydians entered the forest, continuing on in their gradual northeast ascent, and reached the river by nightfall where they bivouacked.

During the night, a small band of supportive rebels intercepted and joined the queen's camp but not before catching their sleeping compatriots by surprise and causing no little stir among them. However, early the next morning all were grateful to find their numbers bolstered and headed together northward on River Road. The Sheaglow lay to their right and was a wide, fast moving river, especially this time of year. The river had wide rocky banks due to seasonal flooding, and the road itself winded along higher ground through the thin, once-replanted forest. After about an hour, they entered the sheltered gorge formed by Mounts Theodore and Timothy; on both sides, the forest sloped up and away, creating a cool damp, sequestered valley. By midmorning, the company reached a large military outpost that spanned the valley.

Panic seized upon the defectors, as if they thought they would reach the city without contest. A stern-looking soldier approached them and looked them over. "Go on through," he said.

Shocked, the party moved forward.

"Just don't tarry long; Asralon is due to be razed in just four days, by order of our wise king, Nathan."

Other factions had been sent home, but the soldiers had spotted the queen and as ordered, allowed her and her supporters safe passage.

They all passed through unscathed and continued on until late afternoon, when they reached the heart of the neighboring mounts and settled down for the night. One more day of travel, and they would reach their destination. They made camp early and so had much time to regroup. Several were quite fearful and not a few talked about the inauspicious, warm reception from the heavily guarded outpost.

Before nightfall, Luna took a long walk into the forest alone and irresistibly, began thinking about her days with the Yimisa. A certain raw wistfulness gripped her as she revisited those memories. They threatened to make her laugh or cry or to anger her, all at the same time; but very certainly, the nostalgic feeling took her breath away: it was almost asphyxiating. Yes, hard to bear; but equally hard to want to let go. Oh, how she wished to wipe it *all* away! Or did she? And to add to it, she was about to visit another spectre: her hometown! She became utterly breathless and her eyes glazed with a saline veil. She continued her walk, completely engaged in her thoughts until the forest grew dimmer, thus signaling her to return to the camp. As she made her way down, the tantalizing, sentimental weight slowly lifted, and she felt her driving determination course through her being once again.

Nearing the camp, she heard the gathering playing instruments and singing some of their favorite songs. Aretta, seeing their demoralized condition, had inclined her friends to lighter thoughts and stirred up a joyful atmosphere: so urgent did it seem to her that these days be spent in laughter and mirth. Hal was there too, egging them on with his own collection of songs and instruments. Aretta sat in their midst smiling again: it was as if she was a new woman. Luna smiled warmly at the sight, so happy she was to see her "sister" smiling again.

The next day was rather uneventful, and as they ascended further, the forest gradually became dominated by evergreens until the retinue popped out a couple miles from town where the alpine meadow and pasture ground spread out across the hills. Not long afterward, toward mid-afternoon, the city began to rise into view.

From the south, Asralon appeared to be a formidable city. She was circled by a deep trench created by the Sheaglow. The western fork was dug out by the early kings, and a primitive, mostly wood wall circled the city on the inner banks. In the background the royal palace rose colossally out from the ground and towered over the city. Beyond the castle and through the trees, the sheer face of Mount Mihai was visible.

Reaching the city walls, they entered the town through the South Gate, unharmed, with the guards at the bridge having nodded in acknowledgment of the returning queen before opening the way for her party to cross. The soldiers promptly reported her arrival to the king who from then on attentively watched from on high.

When the queen's party entered into Asralon, it looked much like a ghost town. Sure there were many loyalists who had come to the city to assist their returning queen, but it was nothing like it used to be in the days when Anna and Luna roamed those streets. The bustle of men and women working and gossiping and buying and selling was nowhere to be found. Instead, the dejected faces of about seventy peasants, mostly old men, were gathered about in the South Square, anticipating Aretta's arrival (the rest of the men were scattered throughout the city). Their faces barely lit up when they saw their queen now showing a little sign of age, followed by an escort of fifty or sixty bumpkins and yokels who looked as though they never saw a war in their lives. Sure, men and women had trickled into the city to offer their support, but after seeing the weak morale and the lack of skilled soldiers, many promptly returned to their homes. The resistance was numbered, in its entirety, at roughly seven hundred men and four hundred women.

After she greeted everyone with a sincere thank you, the queen was taken to her quarters while the rest were schooled on the general prevailing order. After settling in, the planning would begin, but one and all knew that their only hope lay in Nathan softening his heart.

After Luna caught the gist of things, she followed the unmistakable beating of her heart. She and her mother had lived close to the South Gate, and she had spent many years roaming those streets. Not much had changed, and she felt an irresistible pull to wander about her old neighborhood. Her memories of home were bittersweet. Directly ahead of her lay South Street; she followed it for several blocks and there she passed many familiar shops and homes. She stopped at Greenbrier's old storefront and looked through the window: it was utterly forsaken. Empty shelves, cluttered floors, and a bare window where happy plants once stretched out from their pots and kissed the window remained. She crossed the street and ducked into a narrow passage that divided the buildings; as she looked down the close passage, which was cluttered with boxes and trash, she cringed. For a moment, she blinked and could feel the past coming to pay her a visit. Quickly, she turned back into the broad street and took a deep breath. Looking back toward the gate, she thought that she should return to the others and forget it all, but something was calling to her: something within was craving. Walking a couple of blocks to Market Street and continuing across to her left on South Street, she found herself right outside her old home. Going further along South Street, she walked approximately two more blocks to where she found the tavern at which she used to work. Standing outside, she remembered her last day of work:

She was about to say goodbye to her boss when he said, "Leaving so soon, are we?"

"My shift is over, sir," she replied.

"I guess you don't want to stick around for a double shift like the rest of the loonies, now do you?" he asked.

"No, sir," Luna replied, "one shift is enough."

"Smart girl," he said, laughing. "Smart girl. You be ending up like old Claus here one day, I tell you. And that won't be a pretty sight. He, he, he, he!"

Luna couldn't help but to laugh too, and then she walked out the door.

Continuing on from the tavern, Luna turned left on Bronze Way and ducked into the alley behind Claus's. This was the door from which she had left that night. She followed her footsteps past the first passage, then right: left at the next passage, then straight ahead. She went straight past one passage and then another, until … she stopped dead in her tracks; a sudden fear gripped her. This is where it happened.

Her mind flashed back to the day of her rape. The memories were still raw. Fleeing, she turned and ran to her old home. Luna entered through the back door, which had been thrown from its hinges. Entering within, she saw through the clutter and the dust and the foul odor and remembered how things used to be – how her mother kept her coat on that chair near the fireplace, and even more wistfully, how she felt on those Christmas mornings when mother was up early in the morning baking cookies. As a young child she excitedly ran down the stairs upon waking and jumped into her mothers arms. "It's Christmas!" she used to say as she ran over to the fireplace to see what sorts of surprises awaited her. She was so little then, so sweet and innocent. This place was the world to her. Those were the days when she lived so carefree, before the real ugliness of life reared its head and spoiled the truth.

She glanced over toward mother's bed where she was born on the eighth of January. Tonight was a full moon too, and she imagined for a moment that she could recall that bittersweet night: her mother had told her so much about it that it felt like she was cognitively there. Contemplating her birth and her mother's exuberance, she began to wonder, first looking at her own hands and arms, then her surroundings, 'Am I a really a hero? What is this place? What, these people?' She was thoroughly torn and confused: love, affection, hate, pain, attachment – what were they? She slowly ascended the dilapidated staircase that led to her tiny bedroom. A sense of sorrowful disgust filled her as she thought, bewildered, 'This was my home – but was it really?' Suddenly the possibility that she was ever happy vanished from her mind. Luna began to wonder if she was only fooling herself as a child on those giddy days, just trying to blind herself to the reality that lay carefully concealed beneath a mask designed to shield herself from the harsh truth: the world is a bitter and lonely place, and no one can ever be safe.

She moved into her room and sat upon her bed just opposite the solitary window. Outside she saw two older boys running wildly, chasing each other. She began to cry as she saw their smiling faces. 'They have no idea,' she murmured as her lips quivered.

Luna sat for nearly thirty minutes sobbing, until making her way down the precarious stairs and running out into the narrow back streets. Relieved to be out of those dismal surroundings, she wiped the tears from her face and took a deep breath. She tried hard to turn her thoughts to the work at hand.

By the time she made it back to the gate, that burn returned; something inside was aching to make this stand. Those persistent demons – her nagging fears and self contempt would be dealt with in one swift moment. She put on a bold face and joined in the planning. After about half an hour, she lost interest, something didn't feel right. Luna found a place to retire and slept perturbedly that night. So it was that her long forgotten dream returned to her. The dream repeated only a few times and was incomplete. Each time, she saw the mouth of the dark cave, but she wouldn't move closer. She couldn't dare to see what she feared crouched within. As the night progressed, she saw images of bloodstained knives as well as other grisly sights.

XXXI

THE PLANNING

On the morning of the tenth, Nathan called Obstitrix to his side. He was troubled by a dream that he had the night before:

A dog was barking and snarling viciously. It was held back by an unseen hand. Moments later, the dog was released, and fell to the ground, its head nearly severed from its body.

That much was heard together by Obstitrix, his advisor, and Adem, his second in command. Nathan dismissed Adem on some errand before he finished relating the entire dream to his uncle, following which Obstitrix offered his sagacious interpretation.

"It is a dream about love," he said simply. "There is nothing to fear." Uncle continued his interpretation line for line until Nathan, brimming with excitement, graciously complimented his uncle.

"You must be the wisest man alive," he beamed.

The dream would ultimately form the basis for much of the king's inexplicable behavior on the day after the next.

Both camps planned diligently that day and rested in the evening. Luna had tried to absorb herself in the stratagem but still couldn't make heads or tails of it. Furthermore, the spirit of the resistance was declining, and Aretta could do little to stay the storm.

The plan as it stood by the end of the tenth follows:

In the camp of the resistance they would divide their numbers, now almost fifteen hundred men, women, and older boys among the four city gates. Luna and Aretta were to occupy the King's Gate opposite the palace, and a division of five hundred would be stationed there. The remaining three gates were to be held by roughly three hundred fifty respectively. Only about forty of the horses were prepared for war, so they too were to be divided among the four gates.

During the planning, Aretta explained to her supporters that violence at this juncture, was futile, and that their only hope in checking Nathan's plans was in setting a precedent for their fellow Lydians that although cruel and heartless, the will of the king could not sensibly be driven to an all out massacre of his subjects, and that in the end, solidarity would stay his hand and forestall his designs. But given such odds, Aretta once again gave leave to any who were unsure if they wished to continue their support: many wanted to leave yet few actually backed down.

On the other side, the king's orders were simple. One division of cavalry would be positioned at the King's Gate, another division at the East Gate. The defenders would have to occupy all four gates to blockade the city, and so their numbers would be further reduced by the uncertainty of the approach, thus decreasing the risk of unnecessary carnage. Each of the riders was to carry a firebrand and a sword. They were to simply break through the line, make for the city, set aflame everything in sight, and proceed to the adjacent gate to exit the town safely. Each squadron had its own course mapped out, and prospective backup plans. They were ordered to try not to kill anyone and at all costs, to stay clear of the queen. Nathan, having his own plans, ordered Adem to remain at his side.

"We," he explained, "have other business to attend to." He explained his plans to Adem who eagerly awaited the day of the storm.

The following day, the mood was solemn and subdued on both sides. Many passed the time by playing board games, playing music, or telling stories. Aretta had urgently sought, both that day and the day before, to sit in counsel with her son but was rudely refused however hard she pressed. She waited anxiously for replies to her letters, messengers, shouts; the common reply was "I will speak to my mother on the morning of the twelfth."

By mid-afternoon on the eleventh, Luna found her intensity building. Perhaps it was a natural fight or flight response; or perhaps it was her own determination, but something – what she could not say – some kind of exhilarating wave overcame her, and in the wake of the incredible liberating energy that bolted through her, she felt herself enthroned atop the crest of an enormous, powerful wave, which seemed to have the promise to carry her to fulfill her destined purpose. Little did she know, but an intuitive rush was preparing her for her most triumphant moment.

The night fell upon them all, and soon Luna found herself fast asleep, still wearing the same pretty dress she had worn that day.

An enchanting voice whispered softly to Luna. "Come – come and see."

All around Luna, tall grasses waved in the night breeze. Luna looked around to see from where the voice came.

On the edge of the earth she spotted a bluish-purple silhouette of a sleek, lovely woman, floating, with a pure white resplendent light marking the edges of her graceful figure. The light shimmered through her sheer, silvery-white gown that constantly flowed like waves from her feet to her head. Looking closer, a fringe-like sleeve dangled loosely from her shoulders and curled upwards near her elbows, waving in the same graceful rhythm as her gown.

As Luna ascended the hill toward the figure, the bright full moon emerged slowly above the silver, diamond-studded tiara atop the mysterious woman's head. Her long voluminous dark-blue hair floated about her lovely face in waves, adorning her with a blue translucent halo. Clear crystal teardrop pendants with silver settings dangled from her ears. As Luna approached, this goddess floated in perfect stillness with her eyes closed and her soft, lush lips of deep blue pursed together in silence.

"Come and see," she repeated as she opened her eyes and lips.

Willing, Luna was transported to near a rock formation and a nearby, tall stone basin, which was carved with a pictural story. Luna's attention became fixed on it, but she struggled to make out the shifting images. The basin was about waist high and filled with water. She bent over the basin and looked deep inside. There in the still waters she saw that goddess staring back at her. The lovely woman smiled coyly, disturbed the water, and turned away.

Following her departure, a darkness slowly crept over all, enveloping it. Luna began to grow anxious as the peaceful feel of the dream left her entirely. Upon turning around, she saw the empty grave of the fallen leopard and shuddered! Quickly she turned about to find the cave and face the snarling beast growling within.

The lightning flashed. Suddenly she could see the leopard in its entirety, all the secret contents of the cave being exposed to her.

Within and behind the crouching leopard she could see herself standing, dressed provocatively in scarlet; in her right hand were chains wound tightly around the couchant leopard's neck and waist. In her left she bore whips that had left tattered welts upon the leopard's face and body.

The last thing Luna remembered before waking was the cackling grimace of the scarlet lady; this final image shocked her to the core.

XXXII

COMPROMISE

On the morning of the twelfth, before the sun had risen above the surrounding mountain peaks, the resistance awoke to see the eastern ridges delineated by the red fringed sky. During that dawning, as the darkness slowly cleared and the shadows gathered more and more distinction, Asralon began to stir. All the company prepared themselves for their dreaded encounter: all but one.

Luna didn't move from her place; during the noisy morning bustle she was roused from her sleep and sat up on her mat in shock and perplexity, soaking in some kind of mysterious divergence while everyone else rushed to their posts.

At the King's Gate, upon the bridge, the throng gathered and pressed in close to one another, forming a human wall between the gathering cavalry and the city gate to their rear. A smaller crowd blockaded the opening near the gate and stood firmly in their places while about a dozen horse stood to the sides, ready to pursue and attack if the king's army advanced too far. After the cavalry was fully assembled and near the appointed time – an hour after sunrise – Aretta stepped forward and spoke to the commander.

"You don't have to do this," she explained.

"What would you have me do?"

"Order your men to stand down! Nathan's clearly mad."

"A lot has changed since you've been here. Our security stands on the edge of a knife, and now I'm staring at the brink of a civil war. How many people will have to die before you finally realize that it is hopeless?"

"I can't let you go any further. Don't do anything foolish, I beg you."

"Too late, Lydian queen," the captain ended as he brought his horn to his lips. "Brrrrrrruurrrrrrrr!"

The leading men shuffled their horses from side to side, waiting to see who would advance first. A few of the stallions bucked and snorted, while others pawed at the ground. Then suddenly, a surge of energy swept across the lines; the black, chestnut, and appaloosa chargers whinnied and bolted suddenly.

The front line drew their swords and made for the bridge. They formed a "V" to cut their way through the crowd, and on their heels were riders with their lit firebrands.

Luna however, was still back in the heart of Asralon, in the central square; she had, in fact, been there, since she woke up, searching for that fiery spiritedness that had animated her during the past few days. Something had completely changed.

'Am I going to miss my chance?' she worried. 'What am I supposed to do? Will I ever break free of this curse? Should I just go and join the others?'

As she sat there pondering these things, she looked around at the familiar sights. Something touched her deep inside, right at her core; and she suddenly realized that this was the last time she'd ever set eyes on her hometown.

She was here for something else: it was time to look at *everything* one last time. While everyone gathered for the futile battle, she got up and strolled about the city streets. As she made her way towards the more familiar sights, she pictured them engulfed in flames: it was time to say goodbye. She used her last few moments with those places from her childhood – the old inn where she grew up, the tavern in which she worked, her cousin's house, Greenbrier's, and the maze-like labyrinth of streets and alleys, teeming with bittersweet memories – filled with gratitude for the way they loved her, raised her, nurtured and sheltered her. Returning to the central plaza, she spun around with her arms stretched out wide and her head held high, smiling, as tears of joy streamed down her cheeks. 'I'll miss you,' she whispered.

At last, bursting with gratitude, she shouted, "I love you!"

Just then, her eyes caught sight of the replica of the solar system that sat in the great central square. The inscription, which she remembered too well read:

> *Seasons change;*
> *The moon will wax and she will wane;*
> *At the end of day, you remain;*
> *Seasons change.*

She smiled fondly and kissed the ground on which she stood. After that, she packed up her things before suddenly remembering her comrades. She grew concerned for their safety; they would need her help.

She began to run toward her post, but it was too late. The soldiers had cut their way through the throngs of resisters, trampling many beneath the hooves of their steeds. Fires began to spread all around the city, while many of her comrades were desperately clutching at the horses and their riders, being dragged about the city in their attempt to throw a horseman to the ground or take his implement of destruction. The few horse belonging to Aretta's faction had hardly the skill or the numbers to forestall the malignant inferno. And few who ventured back into the city to defend it, made it out alive.

The horses swarmed through the city like a cloud of locusts. As the fire spread greedily, the buildings began to buckle under the weight of their own rooftops and collapse into the streets below.

The streets became littered with flaming walls and timbers as Luna shouted to her friends to guide them through the nearby Sheep Gate. After helping a horde of women and their boys across the river to safety, she stood at the edge of the town, waiting to see who would emerge. The cavalry were assembled and loomed mercilessly beyond her, also watching.

Soon she saw Aretta emerge, her body blackened from smoke and her garments scorched by fire. Hal was close behind her leading a pair of younger ladies to the bridge.

Suddenly, the bridge caught fire and began to burn. Aretta and Hal rushed across among the large crowd vying for safety, before the bridge finally collapsed into the river far below, and all chance of escape was cut off for the remaining crowds who pressed their way forward, inadvertently pushing each other into the river while the others were swallowed by the flames or buried in burning rubble.

The horsemen looked on at the cluster of dispirited survivors who numbered about three hundred altogether. One elderly soldier called out from atop his horse, "Run!" as he slowly lowered his torch to light one of the stacks of dry grass that were placed at close intervals throughout the field. Before the stack even lit, the survivors already began frantically dispersing across the fields and away from the city into smaller and smaller groups as they fled from their new threat.

The tinder grass ignited quickly, and crawled low to the ground before reaching the next stack. Sometimes, a gust of wind carried clusters of charred debris and sparks too; so the fire multiplied exponentially after the first few stacks were lit.

Just outside the city sat a lovely field abloom with rapeseed, daffodils, and pheasant's eye flowers. The yellow and white flowers dotted the meadow grasses everywhere, and those beauties had nowhere to run. The deflecting Lydians fled straight through that bright and cheerful population, until leaping over or passing through the gaps of the low stone wall in the distance that long ago, before the river was diverted, served as a foundation for Asralon's earlier defensive wall.

Meanwhile, Luna, and soon afterward, Hal and Aretta, made their flight in that general direction as well. Luna, starting first, hurriedly walked toward the outlying hills. She covered about half the distance to the wall before Hal and Aretta emerged from the dispersing multitude. Here, amid the spreading flames and the south blowing wind, Luna stood and faced the wind. She took a deep breath, and moving her hair to the side looked around, pondering, as if the air itself was speaking to her. With a slight downward glance, she noticed the pretty flowers spread about the field. She paused and affectionately stooped down low, watching in wonder. Not far away from her, she saw the fair yellow pheasant's eyes disintegrating and disappearing with the smoke. The flames crawled up the length of the stem before touching the soft pedals. As the fire burned, the flowers turned to black before suddenly disappearing. Watching, her senses were overcome and seemed to become intertwined with the dying flowers. Repeatedly, she followed the course of the flame and became vicariously, first one, then another of the dying flowers; and after being devoured by the passing flames, an electric joy began to buzz within her. Every one of the flowers blossomed in its carefully chosen place; of all the places in all the world to grow, they chose to grace the world with their beauty *here*, in the outlying field of a burning city, each of them a willing volunteer to the conflagration.

Suddenly, released from the flowers' spell, she stood up and noticed the flames had caught hold of her dress. She smothered the flames in its folds, but not before being singed on her thigh. Turning away from Asralon, she walked boldly toward the nearby wall, and crossing over, she reached safety, well beyond the reach of the aspiring fire. There, Aretta, having searched her out, finally reached her; yet she had to traverse the entire field of burning grasses, and everywhere she went, the creeping flames licked at her bounding heels.

But that was not all. Earlier, at the King's Gate, moments after the cavalry broke through Aretta's lines, her son approached her with Adem at his side. They circled her threateningly from the tops of their horses:

"Mum!" Nathan shouted jubilantly. "You made it. Oh, I'll never forget the days growing up with you. Here we are again, same old, same old.

"You never knew how to compromise, did you?"

Aretta was silent.

"Look at you. Are you ready now?"

Her silence continued.

"Oh well, what do I know?

"You know, I never could stand it the way it was when you and dad ruled. I can't say I like this all that much either, but what really is there to like anyway?

"Oh well, I had fun while it lasted, and for nearly ten years, we all had the time of our lives.

"Ah, the benevolent face of the state," he continued. "Where would I be without it? You're always welcome in my realm, Mum, don't forget it."

Following her son's upbraiding, Aretta's thoughts turned toward Luna. She hadn't seen her gathered earlier and grew concerned for her safety, so much did she long to see her again. Aretta turned away from her son and ran straight into the burning city. As she rounded the familiar corners, dodging rubble and detoured by the collapsed buildings, she made her way toward the center of town. En route, seeing the hopeless condition of the town, she realized that *she* had to get out. A feeling of hopefulness was kindled in her heart, and she ran hard, leaving her crumbling city behind. Catching sight of the gate, she ran toward it and after attaining it, emerged charred but renewed. The noise of cracking timbers and dying screams lay behind, and ahead was a wide open field of boundless space. She pressed forward with the liberated throng and crossed the burning bridge.

Off in the distance Luna began glowing with an aureole light. Here, Aretta crossed the sea of flames and made it to Luna's side.

"I was a fool, Luna," Aretta confessed.

"I thought I could make everything okay, that I could take away all the pain. I could have learned what I know now, so many years ago, but I chose to live in fear. Afraid it seemed that I could do something hurtful, be a villain; but truthfully I was afraid to give up my illusion."

Luna embraced her warmly. During her flight through the burning field, Luna was utterly transformed. After the last piece fell into place, she saw the world with an uncanny clarity. Her confidence was intoxicating and her inner light disarming.

"It's alright, child," Luna assured her. An understanding smile crept over Luna's face. "But you already know that."

"Even in your foolishness, you held truth. Do not despair. Naught is lost."

Stepping back, Luna placed both of her hands upon Aretta's shoulders. Luna looked intently into her deep-blue benevolent eyes and said, "Go on, Lady Esharah, live like you've never lived before."

"I will," Aretta quietly said as she walked off toward the wilds.

XXXIII

FREEDOM

L una turned to face her final task. An illusory fear was still clinging – though precariously – to the fringes of her skirt, and she was determined to shake it once and for all.

She watched from her height as Nathan and Adem approached her on horseback with a slow train of about twelve young women and several dozen foot soldiers following. The young girls were found among the disordered fleeing multitude and being considered among the best, were picked out by the men to serve their own salacious desires. From the north, the retinue advanced south alongside the ancient stone wall. Luna remained still and calm and waited upon her hilltop.

When the party arrived, Adem descended from his steed and approached Luna to seize her. Grabbing hold of her with one hand, he reached with the other for the rope dangling at his side – to bind her; but as he reached he felt a warm sensation on his neck. Looking up, he saw the stone-cold eyes of the huntress fixed upon him. In her left hand she bore his own dagger now plunged deep into his throat, and the warming that he felt was his own blood trickling down his neck. Luna drew the dagger from his neck and Adem collapsed instantly.

Startled, the company of foot soldiers deliberated before one of them stepped forward to seize her. Before he could move any further, Nathan ordered his men to halt.

She was the one. In his dream, a woman with a chilling glory slew his trusted dog. Uncle had fully recounted the import of the dream to him; and from that moment, Nathan had eagerly anticipated this very encounter.

He descended from his horse and ordered his guards to set the prisoners free. The young women all dispersed into the surrounding country while the soldiers were ordered to return to their posts.

He approached Luna, still bearing the dagger, raised in her left hand. Nathan, almost kneeling, stretched out his right hand in front of his bride to be, and as she reached out and grabbed hold of it, the fear she had long tried to purge from her heart vanished into darkness.

Aretta had turned about when Nathan approached to watch the whole affair. She smiled approvingly as Luna began to mount Nathan's steed. There, Luna looked back in Aretta's direction as a coy smile graced Luna's lips.

Be thou firm and tenacious, and yet changing as the moon;
Live deliberately, oh fleet-footed lover ruling the stars;
Be thou rich in expression yet secret and sublime;
A mystery unfolding, pure, innocent and divine.

A NOTE FROM THE AUTHOR

A few of my reviewers asked if there was going to be a sequel to *Aretta's Gift*, or perhaps, a series. I told them that there would not be a sequel. It is my express wish to never pen a sequel. Things change, but I feel very strongly that some things are best left alone.

In the event that I would produce a sequel, I feel that some of the universal symbolism contained in the present volume would be lost due to the need to adapt the current story to take a more explicit direction. Hence, the material would become unduly individualized, and whatever appeal there may have been in the present story will have been diminished for many of the readers. Furthermore, stories and myths are often best completed by the readers themselves, and the discomfort of not knowing where a story will go is a device of our own psyche whereby further advancement is attained by the ever aspiring self.

The truth is that many of the metaphors contained in the present work are just that, and my audience is quite capable of adapting them to serve their personal needs. After sitting with the sense of incompletion for however long they must, the readers will find that the miracles of "evolution" will have already worked their magic and guided them, *outside of story*, to their own unique resolution.

It would seem that I am in the business of entertainment, but on the contrary, I am not. Otherwise, I should have written a long drawn out series of novels that ultimately caters to an audience who enjoys that sort of art.

No indeed, I am in the business of delivering a story that "gets to the point" and at the same time gives the readers something to work on, yet simultaneously, however covertly, contains all that is required for assimilation. I'm content to leave the writing to the many fine and talented artists who have already graced our world with their eloquent words and unmistakable appeal.

That is not to say that I will never write another novel. Perhaps not. But I love stories as much as the next person; and writing them is a lot of fun, so I'm guessing that I will. However, my greatest desire is far beyond that. On the few pages that follow, the mission and purpose of Osiris Independent Press, which is a vehicle for the aforesaid desire, is concisely stated. Thanks for reading, and blessed be!

Your truly,
Mark J Graver

ABOUT OSIRIS INDEPENDENT PRESS

Osiris Independent Press was formed in response to a desire to "fill a void". I believe that the true power of the people of America is best expressed by the people, and that the founders of our country were entrepreneurs in the most elevated sense possible.

The formula that they followed, first and foremost, being: formulate and clearly express an idea. Having shared that idea, the course of nature will certainly follow. The better the idea, the greater the support. That is not to say that our society will not gravitate toward something "harmful". We will. But the choices we make will – collectively speaking – accurately and perfectly express the direction WE wish to go. Division will assuredly lead to division. Submission, to domination. Inconsistency, to unpredictability and additionally, domination by default.

All said, whatsoever we agree upon will stand because we agree, and the formation of the United States of America was formed due to the agreement present among a group large enough to make a difference.

Using Osiris Independent Press, I hope to find people who agree that the brightest and most sustainable future available to the human race now involves the inner journey and a more concrete understanding of the self. Preserving, exploring, and evolving the vehicle of the human mind and the framework of the human body in its most exalted state are paramount to me. Human potential, aside from what can be accomplished through external means, seems to me the most sensible and urgent field of study both for the preservation of the planet and the assurance of a more enjoyable life.

Everything we could ever need already grows and lives on this planet.

–Mark J Graver

www.ingramcontent.com/pod-product-compliance
Lightning Source LLC
Chambersburg PA
CBHW050946120626
46552CB00001B/403